Gracie,
There are really no such things as dreams. Plans in various grades. Some plans are short, some plans are long term and some seem impossible, but nothing is impossible.

I love you
♡ Daddy
:)

The Reflection of Elias Dumont

J L Carey Jr

BLACK MADONNA PRESS
P.O. Box 183
Otter Lake, MI
48464-0183

Book design by Broken Cog Media:

Copyright © 2016 by J L Carey Jr

ISBN: 978-1-365-38316-8

All Rights Reserved. No part of this book may be used or reproduced in any manner without written permission except in the case of brief quotations embodied in critical articles and reviews.

Contents

Chapter 1 .... p.3
Chapter 2 .... p.17
Chapter 3 .... p.24
Chapter 4 .... p.40
Chapter 5 .... p.53
Chapter 6 .... p.74
Chapter 7 .... p.92
Chapter 8 .... p.108
Chapter 9 .... p.134
Chapter 10 .... p.155
Chapter 11 .... p.170
Chapter 12 .... p.183
Chapter 13 .... p.196

The Reflection of Elias Dumont

J L Carey Jr

Quotes

"I have no terror of Death. It is the coming of Death that terrifies me."

- Oscar Wilde from *The Picture of Dorian Gray*

"I touched her sleeping breasts. / They opened to me suddenly / like fronds of hyacinth. / The starch of her petticoat / made a sound in my ears / like a piece of silk / being ripped by ten knives. / Silver light gone from their leaves, / the trees have gone bigger, / and a horizon of dogs / barks far from the river."

- Federico Garcia Lorca from *The Unfaithful Wife*

"Over head / in a hazy sky / the swirl of clouds / makes a 3 quarter arc / over the moon, /
Below this arc / the moon is dreaming of rain."

- Sam Hamod from *Arriving in Arizona*

Chapter 1

A small lamp stood in the room throwing its harsh light against a young man's face. The light chiseled out the features as it cut down his forehead, flooding its shadow around the left eye before spilling along his cheek bone, jowl and then over the chin. A black bell of a shadow rested on the left side of his nose as well. The shade tolled out a gross representation of Elias Dumont's refined features. At a glance it gave the impression of a skull or a face without its nose.

Outside the hotel window the Mississippi river rose, edging its way toward the Gateway Arch. It rose up, like an untamable serpent against the manmade concrete levies and sandbag barriers that futilely tried to contain it. Elias sat staring out into the gloomy gray mist, his dismal reflection caught in the pane of glass. "I'm sorry," he said softly, "I'm sorry."

A cigarette hung from his pouted lips, its thin shadow meandering down Elias's chin until it just kissed the pool of shadow on his neck. Across the line of his forehead the shadow merged with a mop of black hair that draped over the right side of his boyish face. It curled slightly at the ends, mimicking the smoke that trailed from the cigarette until his jittery hand pushed it back and held it in its anxiety. He mumbled quietly under his breath for a moment as if he were in some secret argument, something about not being mad, something about wanting this to end.

Despite his voice there was no immediate distress about him, there were no wrinkles in his translucent skin; not even a pimple or a blemish. Nothing but the daggered look in his eyes and the rattled tone of his voice discerned anything different. Those eyes though, they revealed a different kind of scarring. They told of something below his polished skin, something that would dispel this façade. In them was that terrible look of loss that the light extracted and played with. It brought it out of the irises in leagues of refracted pain. The light seemed bent on exposing what rested underneath the surface; that anguish that whispered from his lips and vanished into the silent room. The blue and green in his irises screamed as the silver needles of light bombarded them. Each moment the eyes were open was a reliving of every wicked thought, decision or act. Still, they remained open, eyebrows furrowed above them.

  A glean shown occasionally in Elias's eyes as he drew the smoke from his cigarette in. It was an odd pleasure that presented itself for just that breath, revealing for a moment a darker truth. It told of a strange desire, a morbid yearning that perhaps this cigarette would kill him. But, Elias knew otherwise and the eyes were quick to shift again to that glassy sea, peering out over the modern city with its high-rises, colorful cars and long flat barges, glaring through the murk, the pain and the smoke that curled haphazardly away.

  In front of him, on the small round mahogany table rested an ash tray, which he tapped his cigarette against, a bloody bowie knife, a pack of Lucky Strikes with a smear of blood across the word Lucky, a nearly killed fifth of Wild Turkey and the cause of all his

The Reflection of Elias Dumont

problems. It was this Katoptron or small mirror, which now lay face down on the table as Elias grappled with the brutal notion of destroying it. The mirror or more the obsession warred with his better judgment as it had each day since the beginning. Like any fixation it worked to suppress all rationale, to devolve his sense of reason.

Now, his reason had risen up, like the waters of the river, it pushed at the walls that contained it. Today he thought only of ending the pain. He carried this burden, this obsession for too long and in the process lost everything he had ever cared about. Today, he decided, was the last day it would rule him. Today he would suffer no more.

Elias struggled not to look at it. The mirror tempted him constantly, its voice in his ears and spine. It was, to the passerby perhaps, only a looking glass, a small hand held mirror, quite queer and vain for a man to have in his possession. But, to Elias, it was the sustenance of life. He allowed his index finger to lightly follow the intricate carvings on the back of the mirror, the Narcissus flowers that decorated the handle and the outer rim. He felt the reflective faces on the back plate as well; saw them clearly in his mind, the sculpted young man locked in a dream, cursed to stare at his own image forever. No matter how he turned or angled the mirror their eyes were ever locked.

Elias's finger quivered for a moment. His hand, detached from his mind, nearly grasped the handle. The agitated hand jerked away then clutched the bourbon instead. He sent the last of the brown fluid down his throat. It burned in a good way as he tipped the empty bottle again just in case. It was gone, but the scent lingered in his nostrils. The rich smell of bourbon always took him home. It worked like a key to unlock those memories, the myriad of retrospections stowed away in the dark cells of Elias's mind.

So many years he thought and now he found himself close to where it all began; St. Louis, the place where the mirror was lost, where it had slid so venomously into the muddy river, which carried it like any alluvium caught in its rushing brown waters until the thing so brutally deposited itself into his unsuspecting hands. He thought again of that wintry day when the earth shook and the river swelled and everything he loved was altered.

Elias chucked the empty bottle across the room. It made a series of thuds before it came to rest against the leg of the dead bellboy. "What the hell are you staring at?" he shouted. "I know what it is," he hissed, "but you can't have it. No one can," he reeled. "I mean to destroy it." Elias stood for a moment, his chest heaving. He had grabbed the mirror and was shaking it at the corpse; the dead man's eyes fixed in horror. "Yes, of course," Elias said, sinking back into the dark blue chair. "Perhaps I've been too hasty my new friend, but one can never be too careful."

A distorted face floated across the mirror as Elias turned the looking glass and laid it to rest again on the table. He had inadvertently allowed his peripheral vision to spy it, the leathery face like something mummified. The eyes that looked back were yellowed and bulbous as the flesh around them had sunk and there in its cheek was a hole that festered with infection.

The Reflection of Elias Dumont

He turned his head sharply away as the mirror came to rest. With a flinch, he moved his hand and grabbed another cigarette. He lit the unfiltered Lucky with the smoldering butt of his last smoke and returned his gaze to the swollen river. "The 'Great Flood'," he huffed. "What was it that Mark Twain had said? 'The Mississippi River will always have its own way,' or something, 'no engineering skill can persuade it to do otherwise.' I believe Mr. Twain was right." With his toes pressed against his heal he pushed and slid the leather boot from his left foot and then he did the same for the right. The one boot fell lazily over the other beneath the table.

"Have you ever been to New Madrid?" Elias mumbled, as if the dead bellboy were all ears. "I remember that place, I remember it as if I had walked those streets a moment ago," he continued, the smoke escaping his lips and coiling away.

"I was raised there," Elias admitted with an uneasy smile breaking from the side of his mouth, the other corner clinging to the cigarette. "My parents settled there after leaving France in 1787. My father was a mason in France, but moved my family to America with the idea of breaking into the fur trade. He did well for us, but in that small town he realized quickly that he was many things in one. I remember his hands were always rough and calloused." Elias stated, flicking an ash onto the gray carpet. "He had a great smile, my father, which would extend from his pipe to the other side of his face. My mother both hated and loved the smell of his tobacco. She would complain about it when he was home, but I would catch her smelling his jacket when he was away. They were a fine couple."

He allowed his head to rest against the window as he took another pull from his Lucky. Below, cars moved along Market St. as pedestrians scurried in their daily routines. They appeared unconcerned with the pressing threat of the Mississippi. It occurred to him that the people of this Christian era's 20th century, with all of their technologies, had lost their sixth sense, that natural fear of nature and its destructive ability. Some wore trench coats or business suits and others carried umbrellas, there were families walking in their shorts and dresses and none seemed aware that at any moment their lives could change or end for that matter.

"You're the quiet type I see," Elias said. "I can respect that in a man. Perhaps you would like to hear how I came into possession of this looking glass?" he asked, gesturing with his hand to the mirror as a fly buzzed above his stiffening audience. The unfortunate man sat staring coldly, fixed with that languishing gape. "Yes. I thought you might."

Just then the air conditioning kicked on. It injected a dull hum into the room as the cool air drifted bye Elias from the vent below the window. The luxury carried a hint of mold. "It was an ordinary enough morning in the small town of New Madrid." Elias began as the fly landed on the bellboy's forehead. "I had gone to see my fiancée in town, which from our home was a good fifteen minute walk along the banks of the river. There had been a series of earthquakes that had been terrorizing the good people of our area for some time. The first of which had caused a great deal of structural damage, toppled chimneys, that sort of thing. It kept my father quite busy.

I remember the first quake too well. There was a large roar that woke me from my sleep and then the house shook so that it seemed every joint and joist and beam were coming apart. It pitched me from my bed, into the dark room and head first onto the hard wood floor. I was severely stunned. I tell you friend, I'd had the wind knocked out of me before, but never like that," Elias huffed.

Like the dead stare of the bellboy, the mirror perpetually pointed at Elias. The handle reacted like the needle of a compass would. It attempted to place itself within his grasp as if Elias's hand were polar North. Shifting in the chair, he allowed his head to tip away from the window, his eyes falling blankly on his grim companion. A second fly was now vying for the new real estate causing the first to swirl around in a quarrelsome buzz. It caused Elias to drift off as if the morbid squabble was some kind of hypnotic dance.

The cigarette that had been burning between his fingers was now just a long piece of ash dangling from a smoking butt. The hot end was enough to startle him out of his trance. "Yes," Elias said, dropping the ash again to the dark gray carpet. Blinking, he widened his eyes then looked down to find he had grasped the looking glass again. This time the pane had turned to face him. In the mirror was a terrible reflection. With a gasp, Elias quickly turned it away.

He rubbed his face in agitation for a moment then yelled at the bellboy, "You don't want this sorrow my friend." With a thud, Elias got up from the chair and quickly moved to the nightstand beside the bed, opened the top drawer and shoved the looking glass in beside an old bible. There was a look of uncertainty on his face as he shut the drawer and began ringing his hands, pacing about the room and looking around. "No, no, you do not want this I assure you," Elias continued. "It did seem fantastic in the beginning, yes. But," he exclaimed. "There is not a day that goes by now that I do not wish I had never come to possess the mirror." He pushed his nervous fingers through his hair. "But, I apologize. I am getting ahead of myself," he said, taking in a long deep breath as he held his hair back.

"I believe I was telling you about Aurore."

Lighting another cigarette Elias walked over to the foot of the bed and sat down. His strange audience rested on the floor beside him. "Have you ever truly been loved?" He asked with an earnest expression. "I was loved once," he lamented, rubbing his cheek and chin with the palm of his hand. "As I mentioned, Aurore was her name. I had gone to her house several days after the first earthquake," he continued, his languid green eyes rolling for a moment then peering again at the bellboy. "Her home had not sustained very much damage at the time, as many a person's had. A large group even started to believe that it was the end of days. Many of them, taken with fear as you can imagine, moved their families out of their homes and into the forest outside of town.

Of course, Aurore's father, being a sensible man, had not succumbed to such fervor and so that morning in December I sat with Aurore in the small parlor at the front of their home. I would often sit with her there and pretend to be in deep thought, getting up occasionally to look at myself in the oval mirror that hung on the wall. These episodes were usually followed up with a silly question, a triviality or something to break up the monotony of the day. On this particular morning a fire burned in the small hearth. I remember it because the room was very warm after my walk to her house. I sat with her on their dreadfully ugly floral sofa and in one of these moments of thought I said "Aurore," not really wanting a response."

"Yes Elias?" she replied, placing her hand in mine.

"Aurore, why is it you love me?"

There was a hesitation followed by her giggling remark, her young voice like something from a dream. "Well Elias, it's your looks of course."

"Really? Would you have loved me had I, say, suffered some deformity at birth then?"

"You pay my words no mind, mon amour. Had you been born this way I would have loathed you or worse perhaps. I would never have laid my eyes upon you."

If you could picture it friend, my eyebrows lifted and a smile cracked along my face. "Well then." I told her with a huff. "I should consider myself lucky to have you." Then, I held her tighter to my chest and we lounged in that gaudy sofa. It was, if anything, comfortable I suppose. The couch was nestled perfectly by a window in the parlor. I recall the sun beaming through and illuminating her soft hair, every fiber seemed visible and alive. I ran my fingers through the long dark strands. They glistened like strings of chocolate as they fell feathery out of my fingers. Smiling, she let her warm brown eyes close as if the angels had come and were showing her a piece of heaven," Elias recalled, his eyes closed as his hair fell in front of his face. "I remember tipping my head and placing a very sincere kiss on her forehead. Her skin was burning, or perhaps it was the sun or my own heat, but all I could think about was kissing her."

"Elias," Aurore whispered with a voice soft and lost.

"Yes," I answered, pressing my cheek against her hair.

"I lied before," she said. "I would have loved you had you been born limbless."

"Limbless," I said laughing. "I truly am a lucky man."

Grinning for a time, I lightly caressed Aurore's unblemished skin, running my fingers slowly up and down her arm as I had many times before. The softness of her body was tantalizing. The more I touched her, the more I wanted her. She was flawless.

As I sat there with that precious girl against me, her head lying so tenderly upon my chest, I could feel my heart beating, which is something, regretfully; I have not felt in a long time. Every thrusting pump of my blood drove me to want her more. I tell you my friend the petting grew feverish that morning. I allowed my hand to slide up her stomach and firmly cup her breast. Believe me young man at this point she normally would have pushed me away, but that morning she made no effort to stop me.

You can imagine, I'm sure, how amazed I was. Her breast was so firm and her hair so soft. I ran my face down those luscious strands until my lips met the nape of her neck. The first kiss was light, but I quickly turned to sucking on her delicate skin. Aurore, stirring slightly, caused me to glance up. I found she was asleep. Can you believe she had dozed off? I still think she was faking, testing me perhaps to see how far I'd go.

Frustrated, I let my head fall back against the window again. I tell you – Robert," Elias continued, bending over and reading the bellboys nametag. "Yes, Robert, I tell you I felt quite silly about the whole endeavor. But, what can I tell you. Men and women are quite different animals.

When we both woke up again it was a quarter past three and the earth was trembling. We had napped the majority of the day and rose to the startling sound of rattling cups and cracking beams. The house was of a log design and as the earth shifted it twisted and thrashed the joints and foundation. Aurore's maid, Sylvie, had moments ago left a steaming pot of lavender tea on the coffee table across the room. Aurore clung to me screaming as the earth convulsed. The tea pot and cups clamored on the silver tray until, as if bucked off, they came crashing to the floor. In a panic the maid came bursting into the room."

"Sauze qui peut. Aurore, Monsieur! Monsieur Dumont," Sylvie said frantically, tears streaming from her Parisian eyes. "The house is possessed. It est the devul I know. We must quit this place," she continued, grabbing Aurore and I by the hands. "Why est this appening Monsieur?" Sylvie wept as we stood and shook and followed her out the front door.

Aurore was still crying as she went to Sylvie and clung to her. In the air a fog of dust hung. It hid the where about of those wailing and panicked voices, the injured and dislodged people of New Madrid. Disoriented, I stood there, the women holding one another as a thudding sound came and then another and then several thuds hit the ground. "Monsieur!" she screamed. "It is appening again."

I stepped closer to them. I too believed the earthquake may be happening again and then there was that clap like thunder and a burst of air and dust and the sound of tumbling stones that trailed off as they came to rest. The chimney had fallen. A section of the house had collapsed.

Sylvie combed her fingers through Aurore's hair as she held her. "Oh Monsieur," she wept. "We should run for the forest, like the others. Perhaps it is safe there."

"Yes," Aurore pleaded, her body shivering in the December air. "We have to get away from this," she continued, choking back her tears as her lip trembled. There was a blind chaos that buzzed around them in the sulfurous atmosphere. It stirred Aurore's panic as the earth moved like a rolling wave. "Please, Elias. Please. We must get away."

"No," I said. "It would be better to stay here. Your parents are going to come looking for you and if we run off to the woods they will never find you."

"But, the others, Monsieur," Sylvie argued. 'What if Monsieur and Mademoiselle Vavaseur have gone to the woods, Elias? What if they think we have gone there as well?" she questioned me, the agitation in her voice, in her eyes so profound that I did question my own judgment.

"I don't know, Sylvie," I told her, slipping my arms around them both. "I just think we would be safer here where nothing else could fall on us. In the woods, even the trees seem to be falling."

"Oui," she said lightly. "Perhaps we should sit here and wait for your father and mother," she directed to Aurore, her eyes still saturated with tears and dust and a look of utter helplessness. "It's just… I hear," Sylvie murmured. "I hear the screams of others Monsieur," she said shivering, her eyes looking about, searching from sound too sound in the blinding caustic haze and then she turned her head and pressed her cheek to Sylvie's breast again. We huddled there in that state for god knows how long. It seemed time was lost to us until we heard, somewhere in the distance, the name Aurore bellowed. It traveled through the cold and sulfurous air like a ray of light. It caused the three of us to stir, to smile. I saw hope wash across their faces as Aurore screamed "here father".

"J'ai pensé que nous avons été perdus," Sylvie wept, clinging to my hand as she could just make out the Vavaseur's running towards us.

I told her that I thought we were lost for a moment also as I rubbed her arm with my hand.

"Oui, Monsieur. I thought the lord had come to take us all."

Turning to his left, Elias slid off the side of the bed, kneeling down in front of a black trunk. His bangs fell menacingly about his face, which caused him to look through the strands of hair as he unlatched the lid and flipped it open. "I really thought we were going to die Robert," Elias said with a nervous chuckle, his hands rummaging in the clothes and books. He then turned his focus to the trunk, furrowing along the inside wall until he withdrew a fresh bottle of bourbon. "Ah yes," he cheered. "There is nothing like a good bottle of bourbon. Sometimes I think God made this stuff just for me," he said, reclining against the wall beside his grim companion.

With a wave of his hand Elias shooed the flies away from Robert's head. "Yes, bourbon," he grinned, unscrewing the cap. "It makes me terribly violent though," he admitted as the bottle pressed to his lips and the brown fluid poured down his throat.

Chapter 2

In the dim light of the hotel room evening crept in as Elias sat. To his right was the open trunk and to his left rested Robert, his green vest stained deeply with the blackening blood. He thumbed at the bottle of bourbon for a moment. The silence was terrible. There was nothing worse for Elias than to be alone with his thoughts. There was no end to his remorse. But, likewise, there was no end to his treachery either. He took another deep swig, his lips opening to receive the liquor like a rose bud opening for the morning sun. When he pulled the bottle away, he drew a long stretch of air into his nose and pushed the strands of dark hair out of his face again.

"I have the paper still you know," Elias muttered, breaking the dead air of the room. "It's tucked away in my trunk," he pointed with the bottle.

The man of course made no reply, his sallow face in want of peace. One of the flies, in its misguided nature, returned again. It hovered about Roberts hollow eyes just long enough for Elias to snatch it from the air. He shook it feverishly. There was a muted buzzing in his palm until, with a downward thrust, he flung it to the floor in front of him. The fly lay dazed and twitching.

"It is a copy of the Louisiana Gazette that I was offered by a fellow traveler on the way home from my ordeal," Elias continued, pulling the wings from the fly as he spoke. "It has a marvelous description of the steamboat New Orleans maiden voyage up the Mississippi," he

17

boasted, his head tilting slightly towards the corpse. "The articles, while not entirely accurate, are still demonstrative of the events of the time. There had certainly been a comet that one could view with the naked eye. Aurore and I looked upon it several evenings. It was brilliant as it glowed like sulfur in the starry heavens."

On the gray carpet, the fly twitched and then, in a vain attempt, it tried to fly. What it produced was, but a feeble kind of dance. Elias watched it intently as it wriggled. He wondered if it was trying to understand its new form. Could it? He lifted the bottle again and took another swig.

"Those events changed me Robert," he confessed. "The Gazette doesn't tell of that. No, Robert, it doesn't tell of that. Though, it does capture those days. Many of the days actually when the quakes were happening, but it's the darker things it's missing." There was a glum tone in Elias's voice, something on the edge of reproachful. He didn't want to think about what had happened. So many years, so many lifetimes had passed. Still, he couldn't stop himself from talking about it.

"What the Gazette leaves out is that one-hundred and forty miles or so from where I lived, in the then developing town of St Louis, a very unusual event was about to occur. This event, mind you, may very well have led to all of the following said events if one were to be so inclined to believe in such things. I was half way home from Aurore's when the big quake struck. What hit me first was the silence. There were no animals, no birds singing or flying above and no squirrels chattering as they usually did. There was nothing but silence. It caused me to pause. Even the river appeared motionless as I stood at the edge. Before me my reflection rested in the turbid, brown water. It was frozen there in the stilled Mississippi like some murky ghost of my recent past.

As I stared at the image I noticed the ripples begin to form, the picture deforming as wavelets stretched simultaneously across the surface and then the earth erupted. It was, without question, the largest of all the quakes thus far. The tremor threw me off my feet and as I jostled in the grass and duck weed I saw the river begin to flow. Every second was like a surreal snapshot, my body lifting off the earth, suspending then plunging again. With another jolt I understood the current of the river was flowing backwards as if time were rewinding. There was the blinding roar behind me as the ground opened and the rock heaved and the timber fell.

When it ended I lay numb, swooning. The tremulous earth had left me disoriented, my mind drifting with the fumes and particles of dust around me. The land had metamorphosed and the river was mostly gone save the muddy bed and gasping fish it left behind. I trembled as I rose from the muck. I tried to wipe my nose with my jittery hand, tried to orient myself as the images replayed in my mind and then I saw it.

A moving wall of battue stretched across the horizon. The earth had only opened momentarily, just long enough to suck the water from the river into the gaping crevice and then it closed. It heaved a thick wave of water and debris into the air. There was the silence again as the dark mass towered above me. I closed my eyes, took in a long deep breath through my nose, heard the roar of crashing water as it rushed towards me and then the world was tumbling again.

My body twisted and swirled as the flood cut a new course through the landscape. I was under, and in the darkness, time stood still while debris rushed by. I grabbed as branches swept past me, dead animals and pieces of homes. One branch came like a terrible spear, plunging into my face, the jagged end piercing my cheek before the current tore us apart. I surfaced, the light striking me as I choked and then the stasis again as the brown fluid poured into my mouth, nostrils and into my lungs. Life drifted as I slipped through the silt, the leaves and churning stones. I thought of Aurore, thought I was lost in the curls of her long brown hair, lost as Sylvie had wept. There was the reflection again in the tranquil water, that reflection like a haunting specter. The shade reached for me and as my limp arm reached back I felt it.

The object turned above me as my hand brushed along its side. The thing turned until I felt the brass handle, felt the metal slip into my palm, my fingers taking hold as it went. With a desperate jerk I surfaced. My free hand clawed at the top of the trunk as it spun and bobbed in the violent current. I fought to pull myself on top of it and once I had my chest draped across the lid, my hands clutching the handles. There was the feeling of my lungs heaving, burning and choking and then the darkness came again.

When I awoke I was still clenching the handles of the trunk. It had come to rest in a muddy field as the water subsided and the sun went down. There was only silence. The world was dead save the sound of my faint weeping and the slap of my legs in the muddy weeds. I was freezing, my body shaking as I peeled myself away. Still, I knelt before the trunk. I knelt there in the mud and the cold and sobbed as it all sank in and then everything went black again."

    Pressing the bottle of bourbon against the floor, Elias stood up, stretched, stepped over Robert's legs and walked across the room to the table in front of the window. He held the edge of the curtain with the back of his hand and glanced outside again for a moment, squinting into the grainy light. He then picked the pack of cigarettes up, pulled the last one from the pack and crumpled the pack then tossed it into the small waste can beside the dresser and the lamp. "I'm not sure how long I was out," he said, striking a match and lighting the cigarette. "It must have been quite awhile though, 'cause I was damn close to dead when the Indian's found me."

    He blew the smoke out and flopped into the blue chair letting his arms dangle off the sides for a moment and then he leaned forward and began scratching his head. "Often, I wish they had left me for dead. That's the devil thing about hindsight though, isn't it? No one really knows how these things will turn out, not until the thing is done and the consequences of the action are understood. Then and only then is the lesson learned and we are left to say, what if? Yes, my friend, what if? What if, for instance, you had called in sick today or even taken another person's luggage to their room? You would likely not be in the position you are in now, but don't get the wrong idea, Robert. You could not have helped this and neither of us is to blame for what transpired. We are simply the products of circumstance. It is circumstance that brought the mirror to me and it wasn't until nearly a year after I had held that damned thing and meditated upon it that I came to understand the sheer happenstance behind my coming into possession of the looking glass."

He placed the cigarette in his mouth and pushed the hair from his face then brought his foot to his knee and sucked on the cigarette causing the end to glow and then the smoke began to coil again. "I had noticed a man following me," Elias said as the sun failed and the room grew darker still. "I was in town buying some things for my mother when I noticed him. He was a haggardly looking man with long wiry sparse hair and a jaundice look about his skin. I knew what he was before the mirror even warned me, but I let him approach. I wanted answers.

"Hello," he said.

"Hello."

"My name is William Ferro."

"Yes."

"I believe you have something that belonged to me."

"Well, it doesn't belong to you anymore, does it?"

"No, I suppose it doesn't, but *it* doesn't really belong to any of us."

"Really?"

"Yes, and I believe you know that's true Elias."

I hadn't given him my name and that bothered me. I had the urge to kill him there in the road and the mirror egged me. It told me not to trust him, that he was going to try and take the mirror from me and that I should just cut his throat, but I held the urge back. I had sensed him close before, this stringy man that now stood before me. He had filled my recent dreams and at times I had awakened to find the looking glass in my hand and Ferro's face in the pane. "You want to tell me about it, William?"

"Yes," he said.

Chapter 3

The darkness fell quickly upon the room as Elias sat nipping at his bourbon. The yellow light of the lamp grew more defined as it illuminated the corner of the room where he lounged. From the room beside his came the faint sound of a television, a modern convenience he had never taken a liking to. There was also the sound of children, two of them he thought and for a time he listened as they laughed and jumped on the bed. This playing went on until a knock came at their door. He thought nothing of it until he heard the door open and a man ask were they pleased with their room and had the bellboy helped them with their luggage.

Hearing this, Elias took another swig off the bottle and gently rested it on the table and slid his hand across the table and picked up the knife. He then sat upright in the chair and waited. He waited as the man next door thanked the family and closed the door and walked next to his room. The man knocked three times then paused. Silence. He knocked again and as he did Elias slithered from the chair and walked silently in his stocking feet across the gray carpet until he stood beside Robert. The knife was poised and in the silver sheen was the dark reflection of Elias's face, his eyes narrowed and fixed like that of cat waiting patiently to kill its prey.

The man knocked a third time and then came the sound of another man calling to him, saying never mind Charles. I'm sure we'll find out Robbie took off and went to a movie or something stupid with his friends. You know how young men are these days. The man agreed saying it just wasn't like Robbie and then Elias listened as their heavy feet padded down the hallway leaving nothing but the faint sound of the television again.

Taking a long breath, Elias pushed the hair out of his face then slid the knife into the sheath on his belt and sat down on the edge of the bed. He cocked his head slightly, looking at the dead bellboy and then he smirked. "So, as I was saying. This man Ferro had shown up like some character from a dream made manifest. I was somewhat prepared, as I had told you, for I could sense his being near and the looking glass would assure me of the truth behind these feelings.

We walked for sometime through Cape Girardeau District without saying a word to one another and then he retrieved a flask from his coat and offered me a nip and I thanked him, taking the spirits and then offering it back to him. It was then, as we walked down the dirt road and out towards the water-mill that he began his tale of how he came to lose the mirror.

"It had been a few days since I had eaten," William said. "Videl was close behind me and I knew it. It had taken all of my wits to discourage him, but I was confident that I would shake him that night. I had paid a man that morning for transport aboard a flatboat scheduled for launch at 8:00 p.m. My plan was to take the boat as far south as it would carry me, which the man had told me, god permitting, would be New Orleans.

A fear crawled through me as I sat in a small tavern on Walnut St. just up from where it was docked. It was the fear that Videl was close. As I sat drinking I had the vision once more of Videl's horrible face. My mind reeled as the vision of the man appeared even more decayed than ever before. The worms did not leave his body anymore, but instead infested and devoured it. Somehow still, Videl lived.

"Sir, would you care for another glass of wine?" the waiter said.

"Yes, thank you," I answered with a twitch, sweat beading down my face. "Wait! Actually boy, I'll take the bottle and save you the trips."

"As you wish sir," he said with a nod.

I swallowed the last of my wine and sat the empty on the waiter's tray. The man gave me an obligatory smile then turned and walked away. I sat fidgeting. I pulled my pocket watch out, looked then tucked it away. I scanned the tavern. There were a few men sitting at the bar, their backs turned to me. I pulled my pocket watch out, looked then tucked it away. 6:53 p.m.

Across the dining area from me was a younger couple. Their table was against the gray boards of the wall. They were oblivious to me or to anyone for that matter. The woman never took her eyes off the man in front of her, her dinner napkin folded neatly across her lap. The gentleman only glanced up occasionally from his bowl of soup. He was a tart, I thought. I pulled my pocket watch out, looked then tucked it away.

"Damn it, move faster you bloody timepiece," I cursed under my breath. There was a bit more grumbling, something inaudible from the mirror as I sat, the beads of sweat ticking down my face. "I ought to stab that tart," I mumbled, my hand sliding into my

The Reflection of Elias Dumont

jacket, toying with the handle of my knife. "That would liven things up."

"Here's your dinner sir," the waiter said, interrupting my thought, "and, your bottle of wine. I hope everything is to your satisfaction."

"Yes," I smiled. "It smells delightful," I added. "I'll be drunk soon though, so if it isn't I won't know the difference."

"Very good sir," he half laughed. "Enjoy your meal."

I smiled until the waiter turned, then sneered at him. "That damn fool, I should slit his pompous throat too," I grumbled, cutting into the roasted chicken on my plate. I chewed as I thought of Videl getting closer, sweat beading on my brow. It caused me to become anxious again. I pulled my pocket watch out, looked then tucked it away. A twitch fluttered in my damned left eye as I stuffed more chicken in my mouth. 7:15 p.m.

Taking a deep breath in through my nose, I ground the meat between my teeth, peering out the front window of the tavern. I tell you Elias, I half expected to see that demon walk up to the door from the dirt street. My fingers clamped around the bottle of wine with a slight tremor. It was a large dark brown bottle, a port of some type, perhaps it was something Italian. It was irrelevant. I pressed it to my lips and guzzled until a bit of the red fluid dribbled down the side of my chin. I wiped it coarsely with my linen napkin as I watched the couple across the dining room again.

The waiter had brought out their main course a few minutes ago and it appeared the woman was displeased with her meal. Her hands, beneath the table, were wringing the linen napkin on her lap, her dress suffocating the chair that it enveloped. The clean shaven gentleman sitting adjacent to her, her husband or whatever he was, was unconcerned. He did his best to ignore her as he forked into his steak tartar. Her eyebrows rose as she spoke to him in silent words of futility. The meal was like a recurring dream for the gentleman, one he may have suppressed, tried to forget about, you know the type Elias, but then there he was having it again, the whole terrible thing flooding back in.

With another swig from the bottle, I watched the woman begin to look about the tavern. She grew impatient. I watched her crane her neck, watched as she motioned with her hand to the food, mouthing something else to her now perturbed companion. He shot her a strangling look, dabbed the sides of his mouth with his own napkin then looked towards the back of the restaurant. There was of course no waiter. The doors were now perched motionless beyond the three men drinking at the bar. Even the bartender was unaware of the couple's dilemma as he inventoried the liquor on the shelves.

The waiter had disappeared beyond the bar, through the swinging doors, just as he had after delivering my meal. He was a pompous and inattentive ass, the kind of young man I liked to bump into in a dark alley, the kind I enjoyed relieving of their wallet,

The Reflection of Elias Dumont

their ego or sometimes their life. This all depended on my general mood. The woman twisted her delicate neck to look there as well while the gentleman wadded his napkin and placed it beside his plate. He was about to stand up when the owner walked past my table. It caught the couple's attention, allowing the gentleman to gesture a two fingered come hither.

Gnawing at the bone of my chicken, I watched the owner approach the table, watched him put on his concerned face as the gentleman rubbed his forehead then aimed the open hand at the woman's plate. The woman appeared to be giving him some type of explanation as to why the meal was disagreeable. He watched the owner tip his ingratiating head while picking up the plate. The woman offered a polite smile at the man as he turned; her companion was already unfolding his napkin, already going back to his way of tuning her out.

I tipped the bottle again, my eyes following the owner until he reached the swinging doors of the kitchen. I then rose from my seat, placed my hat on my head and quietly slipped out the front door. Luck, I thought. Luck is when opportunity meets preparedness and this was my lucky day. It was my way after all to leave without paying whenever possible and I believed there was no better opportunity than someone else's misfortune.

It was Videl's misfortune Elias that I thought of as I stepped into the evening, the dimming light, the quiet of the streets of St. Louis. I walked briskly, making my way towards the dock. Videl had lost the mirror, which, I felt had been the luckiest thing that could have ever happened to me. What man would not want immortality I pondered, a sense of gratification filling me as I guzzled from the bottle of wine?

I pulled my pocket watch out, looked then tucked it away as I left the darkened street. The heels of my boots clapped as I strode through the sparse group of people who stood chatting on the wooden planks of the dock. A man tipped his head to me as he lit an oil lantern. It caused my left eye to twitch as I sucked the last of the port from its bottle. I sent the empty brown glass into the water with a hurl. The thudding splash caused several heads to peer into the dark, the shimmering yellow light of the oil lanterns rippled in the agitated water.

I had half a mind to go back and stick the bastard lighting the lamps, the mirror told me to do it, but I put it behind me. I could see the flatboat, hear them calling for boarding. I just needed to put myself at some distance from Videl. I could feel him even closer.

At the foot of the gangway a small group of passengers waited to board the flatboat. I tried not to be anxious, but was failing. As I looked about the dock I noticed a pretty young woman watching me. Ordinarily this would concern me, but for some reason it calmed me. Her eyes were on fire as she sat on the mooring post and stared, her face stoic and emotionless. Her skin caught the light differently. It was something more like wax I thought. She was unreal.

"Are you coming aboard then?" a man said, breaking my gaze.

"Yes."

"You'll find your quarters on the Port side," the man gestured. "I believe your trunk has been brought aboard Mr. Ferro."

"Yes, thank you," I said smiling.

"We should be setting off promptly sir."

With a nod, I walked up the gangway, pausing for a moment to look for the girl. She had disappeared into the night. I thought about how strange she was, so different and then I thought of how she was a lot like me. I let my eyes sweep the pier one last time before I turned and boarded the boat. It was never really safe for me. I never knew who really was after the mirror, but in this tiny cabin aboard a boat heading down the Mississippi, I did feel somewhat more secure.

There was a window in the back of the flatboat, which I paid extra to secure, and I could hear the men outside as they labored to steer the nearly one-hundred foot craft with the long poles. There was also a small bunk with a table beside it, two small wooden chairs and my trunk. On the table an oil lamp burned its whale fat. I shut the door behind me, kicking my boots off before sitting down at the table. I enjoyed the sound of the water and the long poles, the creaking of the timber and the fresh cut smell of the wood as I reclined back, the gentle rocking as we lurched forward and the feeling of being underway.

The swaying of the boat made me sleepy. It always had that effect on me, every time I slipped away to some new part of the world. This time was no different. I slid my knife out from its sheath and tucked it below my pillow. I took off my jacket, un-tucked my shirt and slid the looking glass out from the back of my trousers. Then, I squatted, unlatched the trunk, cracked the lid and slid the Katoptron into the trunk. It was closed and latched again before I really had time to think about it. There was some murmuring though. It didn't like being in the trunk, out of my hands, out of my control. But, I felt safe aboard this boat as I pulled the wool blanket back, slipped beneath it and allowed myself to fall asleep.

In the morning I awoke to someone pulling on my toes. Two goose feathers drifted in the gray light as I sat glaring at a young girl. The knife had ripped from beneath the pillow as I shot from my sleep and into some kind of attack mode. "Who are you?" I belched.

"I'm Paulette," she said softly. "We are going to go ashore soon."

She was harmless. She couldn't have been more than fifteen I thought as I slid from the bed, my feet bracing the cold floor. "Yes, of course," I said apologetically, sliding the knife into its sheath and walking towards the door. She had an awkward smile and a freckled face. In her hands was a small bowl, a pot of hot water and over her arm draped a ragged towel. She tipped her head slightly to one side as she walked towards the table. I began to motion with my hand that I wanted the bowl here, but before I could say anything to the girl there was a crash on the floor as the pot and the bowl shattered into a jagged pool of steam.

I whirled around to see that all too familiar look in Paulette's eyes, that look of shock, of questioning and of death. Behind her stood Videl, the tip of his long

The Reflection of Elias Dumont

knife jutting from the girl's sternum. It made a grisly sound as he slid it out. The girl fell in a terrible heap upon the shards of broken china. She had the look of a doll some child had tossed on the wooden floor.

"It seems you're cornered old friend," Videl jested, stepping inside and closing the door.

I glared at him as I pulled my knife from the sheath again. "One day you'll stay dead Videl," I snickered, eye twitching.

"And do you think today is that day Ferro?"

"Well," I answered, staring into Videl's horrible black eyes, worms popping out of his flesh, then slithering back in. "Perhaps if I cut you into small enough pieces the fish will eat them and I will finally be done with you."

Videl stepped closer. He wore a long filthy coat, a black hat and black leather gloves. He did not attempt to cover his face though. The decomposers of the earth were actively at work, emerging from the collar and then disappearing into his body again. Upon closer look, I realized Videl's body was comprised entirely of them.

"Does my appearance sicken you?" he questioned, his knife rising, pointing at his face. "You're going to pay for burying me alive Ferro," he growled, his eyes dilating as his face seethed.

My own skin crawled as I stepped back, my stocking foot bumping the trunk beside the table. I made the mistake of letting my gaze fall to it. I knew the folly of it as soon as I did it. Videl's gaze also fell to the box, to the yearning of its contents and to its possibilities.

The first lunge came with a swooshing sound that narrowly missed opening up my abdomen.

With a downward swipe, I sheared the breast of Videl's coat. It caused it to flap open like some curtain to hell. Some of the white ribs were exposed as the makeshift flesh pulsed. It made no difference to the demon as he stepped forward again, his second lunge taking my fingers off at the knuckles.

Gasping, I saw time take hold of the finger tips, saw them age and wither on the wooden floor. I knew the fingers that now sprouted out of my hand were something else, some mirage for the world to behold, something unreal and inhuman. The knife came at me again for a third time, gleaning in the gray light. With a desperate gesture I swung my own knife again. It caught Videl's blade with a crisp clang, but the motion caused me to fall against the table.

I saw Videl step back, his chest heaving. There was a darkening look of determination in his eyes as he readied for another lunge and in a moment of haste I flung the oil lamp at him. The glass shattered on Videl as it struck him, the flames rushing with the oil as it doused his face and coat. There was the disturbing sound of insects screeching in some high pitched wail. It caused Videl to let out a loud cry as he flailed, the flames spreading to the floor and walls.

This was my only chance. Twisting, I grabbed the trunk from the floor, opened the window and flung it out. It went perilously into the deep muddy water of the Mississippi. I then placed a foot on the table and prepared to leap myself when I felt the knife. The swipe severed my Achilles' heel as my hands grasped the

The Reflection of Elias Dumont

window jam. I felt the burn in my leg as the muscle retracted, felt the sting again as the knife plunged into my back and then the world was in flames as I sank into the burning cabin.

It did not take long, even in the cold December drizzle, for the boat to become engulfed in flames. The fire rose along the Port side of the flatboat, lapping towards the gray sky. Many of the panicked passengers dove into the icy water. Within minutes the river had taken control of the vessel. As the Port side collapsed the boat careened in a churning inferno, caught a rocky crag on the shoreline then tore into pieces.

I thought, as I lay on the floor watching the flames curl from Videl and the ceiling and planks on the walls, that I was doomed to burn alive and in that moment I realized the justice of it. I was certain that I was sure to get that which I had given so many times. But then the craft tore apart and I felt the cold rush in and then the darkness swallowed me as the undertow pulled me into its murky hell."

Ferro handed me the flask again and as I watched the wheel of the mill turn I tipped the container back and drank, then replaced the cap and handed it back to him. His hand trembled as he took it from me. There was a stink about him that the breeze mustered also. It was the smell of something rotting, like the smell of a dead mouse. The smell oozed from his mouth as he spoke.

"You must destroy the Katoptron, Elias."

"And why would I do something that foolish?"

"Because, it is the only way to stop this; to end our suffering."

I turned away from Ferro as he was speaking and looked into the sky. It was a brilliant solid blue with just a wisp of cloud to the north and nearly above me the sun hovered, its warmth streaming down onto my face. I had no intention of destroying the mirror. At the time I was so full of myself and the looking glass had a way of fueling my vanity as well as my self-assurance. And so I turned to him again and told him I agreed. A grin cracked across his haggard face exposing his rotting teeth and then he unscrewed the cap of the flask with his nubbin hand and made a toasting gesture before tipping it back. I thought of how he had described the fingers as they fell away from his hand and then I returned the smile.

"Come into the mill Mr. Ferro. I have something I want to show you there."

"Yes," he said. "What is it?"

"I believe it's something you will be interested in."

"Well, let's see it then."

He took another nip from his flask and then he offered it to me again as I passed him. I thanked him and then took the flask and tipped it as I walked. He followed close behind me as I stepped onto the wooden planks of the porch and opened the door to the mill. William stepped inside as I held the door and I followed, closing the door again and handing the flask to him.

The Reflection of Elias Dumont

Inside the rush and the fall of the water as the giant wheel turned was slightly muted, but the large stone wheel twisted. There was no grain in the hopper for they had finished their grinding for the week two days ago and against the wall their tools still rested.

"So, what is it you wanted to show me?"

"It's there, below the floor. If you open the cellar you'll find something there that belongs to you."

"Is it my trunk?" he asked, putting a knee to the floor and setting the flask down and grabbing the handle. "Did my diary survive?"

"Yes," I told him as my hands grasped the scythe that rested against the wall and I stepped and swiped. It was a clean cut as his head dropped and rolled and then the body fell as the cellar door fell with a clank and a thud. "But, it's not here."

What I found to be curious was that there was no blood. I bent and picked the flask up from the ground and tipped it as I studied the severed area of the neck. There was instead a powder that puffed from the wound, something that looked more like rust. It was a fascinating thing I assure you and it took me some part of the day to chop his body up and carefully feed it down the hopper and into the grinding wheel, all along that powder filtering out of the stone and into the catch basin.

There were a few times that I could swear I caught his eyes watching me, his mouth in some silent scream as I rolled my sleeves and went about my work. Once they even seemed to plead, even weep and were there an ounce of moisture in his flesh they may very well have. But, of course I couldn't stand to look at it so I placed the thing in a grain sack.

When it was all finished I placed the tools back against the wall and carried the catch basin outside, shaking it with the wind as I walked until I had properly scattered the remains. Then I went back to the mill and set the basin back in place and grabbed the grain sack and carried it home. I tell you, I thought about keeping it. I know that's strange, but it had a war trophy sentimentality to it. William was the first of them to go and I was quite pleased with myself that my plan had gone successfully into action. The looking glass advised me better though. It demanded I to get rid of it. So, that night I burned Ferro's head and buried the skull and ashes in the woods beyond my backyard."

Getting up from the bed, Elias stood and stretched and rubbed his fingers in his eyes then he walked over to the table, bending and grabbing his boots. "Well, my friend," he said slipping his boots on. "If I am going to tell you this then I am going to need some more cigarettes." He stretched again and scratched his chest then he moved along the side of the bed to the night stand, opened it and took out the looking glass. His eyes focused on the bible as he tucked the mirror quickly into the front of his pants, tucking his shirt in over it and then he turned and went to the lamp and shut the lamp off.

"Can I get you anything?" he asked Robert as he passed him in the dark room. A dead silence followed as if the world had been momentarily muted. "Suit yourself," he said, opening the door, stepping out and then closing it and trying the lock. He pressed his plastic key card in, withdrawing it quickly as the small green light clicked on and then he cracked the door open again; the do not disturb sign swaying side to side with the movement of the door. Elias shut the door then and tried the lock again, repeating this several times before turning and pausing and leaving.

Chapter 4

Outside the hotel, Elias stepped onto the sidewalk and inhaled the evening air. Its scent was rich with a dank moisture; a moisture that steadily filled in the city around him. He walked for a time with his hands in his pockets until he reached the base of the Arch and then he stood looking up at it. The metallic structure towered above him in its beautifully useless way. Streaks of silver light broke across its plated surface like bands of lighting. The whole structure seemed to capture the city and then distort it. He took the air in again as a breeze carried the smell of the Mississippi river to him. It caused him to shudder.

The swollen river's banks had nearly reached the base of the Arch and as he looked out and across he pulled his hand from his pocket and felt the handle of the looking glass beneath his shirt. Part of him wanted to fling it into the river, to cast it away, but he knew the futility of this too well. It was certainly not the answer and he understood that better than anyone. His hand trembled as he pulled it away and tucked it back into the pocket of his pants. He looked again at the water, at the lights of the city muted in its pungent darkness and then he turned and walked to the road and hailed a cab.

A red Laclede Cab stopped and then he opened the door and slid in. "I need to go to a liquor store."

"Any particular one?" the cabby said glancing back at Elias in the rearview mirror.

The Reflection of Elias Dumont

"Doesn't matter, but after I stop there I'd like to go somewhere to get a drink."

The cabby nodded as he depressed the meter and then accelerated into the sparse traffic. "You from around here?"

"It's been a while, but yes."

"You don't look like the club type."

"No. Is J & A's still around?"

"Sure."

"That'll be fine."

The man nodded again and made a turn onto Olive St. and headed west until he reached a party store, then stopped. He waited with the meter running until Elias came back out and then they drove on again, past St. Louis University and onto Lindell Blvd. until they reached the Central West End. Elias sat staring out the window, the lights and the buildings passing as he tapped the pack of cigarettes on his knee.

"You been gone a long time then?" the cabby asked, but it was rhetorical, something to break the sound of the tapping perhaps.

"Does it matter?"

"No," the man said, scratching the stubble of his face. "Just trying to make conversation is all."

The cab slowed and then they made a left turn onto Newstead and drove a few blocks until they reached the old brick building that stood on the left side of the avenue. Elias pulled a money clip from his pocket as the cabby slowed and stopped along the west side of the avenue, turning his body slightly as his elbow rested on the back of the bench seat.

Pulling several bills from the money clip, Elias handed the man his money and told him to keep it. The cabby thanked him as Elias opened the door and stepped out onto Newstead Ave. and shut the door and then he walked across the avenue, stopping beneath the street light for a moment as the cab pulled away. He looked around, lingering, resting against the black iron pole as the artificial light exposed him, like a lighthouse would above some foreboding shore where shallow jagged rocks lie hidden below deceptively tranquil waters. He was patient as he stood lingering, calculated and after a few minutes passed he glanced up at the small sign that jutted out from the brick just above the shingled awning and then Elias opened the pack of cigarettes and threw the foil on the ground and popped one out of the pack, placing it in his mouth and lighting it.

As he opened the squeaky door he stepped into the dim neon light and let the door slam behind him. There were more people in the place than he thought there would be, but that wasn't saying much and after quickly scanning the bar he moved towards a corner seat where he could face the door. The bartender nodded at him as he passed and Elias returned the nod and blew the smoke from his mouth as a waitress approached, greeting him as he sat down. He slid the ashtray closer to him and tapped his cigarette on it.

"What'll you have hun?"

He smiled at her and tapped his cigarette again, "A fifth of bourbon and a glass of ice."

The Reflection of Elias Dumont

"Tough day at the office then," she said with one hand on her hip and the other pressed against the table.

"Something like, that."

"Well, you ain't plannin on driving home tonight are yah?"

"No ma'am."

"Good," she said turning and strutting towards the bar.

He leaned back in the seat and smoked and watched the door and as the waitress came with the bourbon and the glass he saw the door open and close. In the doorway stood the silhouette of a woman, as if the shadow of something beautiful had entered and paused, but it was no shadow. It caused the bartender to look twice. She stood motionless for a moment, some fragments of light still filing in behind her, lucent stragglers, enough to keep the faint aura around the figure until she eased forward.

"Let me know if there's anything else you need, hun," the waitress said as Elias poured the bourbon in the glass.

"Thank you. I will."

He swirled the ice and the bourbon in the glass keeping his eyes focused narrowly on the woman who seemed to move like liquid through the yellowish light and dense smoke. She seemed the only thing in the room that could truly move freely, uninhibited by the elements of the room, the tables, the chairs all fixed in their places. Even the dim xanthous light over the bar appeared trapped as if a hundred years of thick smoke had somehow slowly dried it into a jerky like substance, its particles condensed and the light suspended in time. Yes, suspended in time he thought as he made a final swirl with the glass and shot the brown fluid down his throat.

The cold bourbon had a better sting and as he sat the glass back on the table he placed the cigarette into his mouth, then he pushed the chair beside him out with his boot, looking up as he raked the hair from his face. In front of him stood the woman. She had her arms crossed and her head tilted slightly to the side and as she stood there her long brown hair delicately coiled and fell around her bare shoulders. Elias marveled at her as she glared at him, her green eyes glinting slivers of silver.

"Sit down, Echo," he said as his eyes flowed along the curves of her blood red dress.

"Why did you come back, Elias?"

"Is that any way to speak to an old friend? Sit down."

With some reluctance she scooted the chair in and sat down beside him. She let her arm press against his arm and then he placed his hand on her hand and felt her cool olive skin. With her free hand she took the cigarette from his mouth and leaned in and kissed him and as she pulled away the smoke lingered between their lips and then she placed the cigarette in her mouth.

"You're still trying to kill yourself," she said, "and I'm still trying to live."

His eyes said what his lips failed to say. He just smiled as his eyes filled with pain, like two pools of terrible anguish that were trapped in this façade, two pools of turquoise suspended in time. He may have wept had the waitress not shuffled up to their table.

"That's a gorgeous dress," the waitress said, "What'll you have?"

"Thank you," Echo said softly, her eyes remaining fixed on Elias.

"What's your name?" Elias asked.

"My name is Jaime, hun."

"Jaime," he said, his face softening. "Thank you, Jaime. Could you just bring us another glass of ice?"

"Sure thing, hun."

He took another cigarette from the pack and lit it as the waitress went to the bar and leaned over the counter to grab a glass, filling it with a scoop of ice. In a moment she had returned smiling, setting the glass on a napkin. They exchanged smiles as she quickly slid the glass in front of Echo and then she started across the room to another table. Elias watched her. He noticed how she seemed to walk with purpose, so much more animated than Echo or he, so much more alive.

There was something familiar about her, he thought, but he could not place it. He watched as Jaime placed her hand on the table she had gone to, a square table with its cheap veneer peeling at the corner and curling, where three men sat brightening as she spoke, her hand resting as it had on his table earlier. It occurred to Elias, as his mind drifted with her every move, that by doing so she openly laid claim to it, as if each table were a moon in which to place her flag.

The sound of Echo's voice played in his ear as he watched the lips of the waitress move silently, her flirtatious mannerisms, her eyes as they smiled playfully at the men and the wisp of curly hair that fell from her ear and down her cheek to her neck so strategically loosed from the pony tail that held the rest back. He watched as two of the men leaned in closer to her and the other sat back and spoke and then the four of them laughed. And then he noticed her place her hand on her hip again and how she pushed her chest out, her breasts full beneath the black t-shirt as she laughed again. Everything about her was alive. Everything about her, every sensuous and awkward gesture finally reminded him of Aurore.

"You like her?" Echo breathed into his ear, a torrent of memories washing over him.

"She reminds me of someone. That is all."

"A woman you loved?" she said, her manic-like hand growing tighter on his inner thigh.

"She was," he said with the drink swirling in his hand and his gaze fixed on the waitress. "But of course, she's dead."

"How did you know I would be here still?"

"You're a creature of habit, Echo. You have been here for as long as I have known you."

"I saw you outside, you know," she grinned.

"I thought you might."

"And what if I were gone?"

"You weren't."

"But, what if?"

"Why do women get into these kinds of conversations?"

"And men don't?"

"No. Well, not usually."

"Tell me about this fiancée," she smiled. "Was she as pretty as this, Jaime?"

"I don't want to talk about her."

"Did you kill her?" she continued, her voice hypnotic as she placed a faint kiss upon his earlobe.

The mirror growled in the back of his mind, beckoning him to kill her, to thrust his knife into her heart, but he sat and drank and stared at the waitress who had turned from the table where the three men sat. She was laughing and rolling her eyes to the bartender as he rubbed the stubble of his shaved head. The man looked to be in his mid forties, the short stiff hairs a salt and pepper from his crown to his chin except the mustache, which plumed thick and patchy gray on his lip. She made a gesture to him as he craned his neck forward slightly over the bar and then he poured a pitcher of Bud Light and sat it at the edge of the bar for her to pick up.

She grabbed three mugs by the handles with one hand and placed three napkins and the pitcher in the other and started off again, back to the table with the three men. The man at the far right had his money ready for her as she sat the beer down and leaned over the table to place the napkins and the mugs and when she straitened again she placed her hand on the man's shoulder. Smiling, he handed her the money. She said something to them and they laughed again as she pulled some money from her apron and handed him his change. He gave her a dollar tip then she skirted on to another table.

"Your skin is so cold," Elias said as Echo slid her fingers over his hand, a hand that had involuntarily grasped the handle of his knife as the mirror quietly urged him to drive it into her heart.

"Yes," she said, her eyes gleaming with silver as they violated his mind. "I just need something to warm me up."

She slid her hand from his, fingernails grazing the skin and placed it on his thigh and then Elias let the handle go. The looking glass repeatedly beckoned him not to trust her. He could hear its low whisper in the back of his mind, but he pushed it back, further into some dark and muted recess. It wasn't going to rule him anymore. He wasn't going to listen.

With a smile, Elias poured the bourbon in her glass and then he filled his glass and sat the bottle down again. Echo looked at the glass and back at him and then smiled with that smile of hers, a smile that never quite revealed her teeth and yet the lips were just slightly parted. She tapped her cigarette on the ash tray and as she did he picked her glass up and drank it then filled it again.

"Do you ever get drunk?" she asked as she pressed the spent cigarette out on the small copper colored ash tray.

"No," he said, swirling his drink for a moment and then tipping it quickly back, the ice clattering as he sat the glass back down on the table. "Or, maybe I do, I don't know. It's been too long. I can't remember not being without it. Hell, maybe I'm drunk all the time," he continued, grinning as he filled his glass again.

She was beautiful he thought as he looked at her, a gorgeous instrument of destruction. He felt her cold hand on his thigh as he drank one glass after another, as the brown liquor dwindled in the bottle and the smoke coiled and saturated every particle in the bar and his mind clouded and drifted to that long ago place when he had first seen her, caught the transient smell of her like the fleeting smell of a flower just before the petals wilt and fall. But, she was an everlasting flower, Elias thought, an everlasting rose with two hidden thorns of mutilation. He longed to die in her arms. He wanted it more than anything, to feel the embrace of it, to slip into that sleep as her arms coiled around him and drew him in and under.

"It's almost closing time," she said. "I'm going to slip out for a moment, get a bite," she continued as her hand left his thigh and glided to his knee and off. "I'll bring a cab around."

"Yes," he said. "I'll just kill this bottle then."

She turned slightly in her chair and then looked back at him. "I need to know why you left back then, before, why did you leave me?

Smoke drifted from his lips as Elias sat, his eyes looking somewhere or nowhere, at the bar perhaps or the shadowy image of himself in the Heineken mirror on the wall. "I left you," he said, pushing his tremulous fingers into his hair so that the strands stood and leaned like wilting plants. "I left you, because I loved you."

With a grin, Echo stood up, then, with that same fluid motion, left the bar. Elias tipped back on the legs of his chair and put the bottle to his lips, the bourbon stinging as it flowed. He thought of Echo again, of the first time he had seen her. It was summer, 1893, and well into the evening. The day, he recalled, had been dry and scorching and as the darkness fell it remained nearly eighty degrees as the men loaded boxes of Budweiser beer onto the wagon. The last delivery of the day he had thought, hefting another box up, its bottles jingling in the case. Some of the other men laughed as they joked with one another and the horses stirred, their hooves clicking on the cobblestones. Elias drew the back of his hand across his damp forehead and peered across the street as the other men secured the boxes down.

Beneath the moon, in shades of black and blue, a pale woman sat beneath a poplar tree watching him. She had long black hair from what he could tell or maybe the dim light worked spells on his eyes, he didn't know. In the air he caught the faint scent of flowers. He breathed lightly and then it dissipated. Without thinking much of it, he pulled a pouch of tobacco from his pocket, rolled a cigarette and rested it between his lips. As he struck the match he realized the woman was gone. He let it go from his thoughts as he inhaled the rich smoke and turned and gave a menacing look at the draught horses. He could tell they were uneasy because of his presence there. They knew he was no good. They could smell it on him just as he could smell the dread on them. Unlike people, Elias found, animals did not overlook their instincts, nor did they take them for granted and ignore them. Elias smelled their fear like

The Reflection of Elias Dumont

the pungent urine and droppings they left on the cobblestones. The fear hovered in the air around them like the many maddening flies that swirled, brooded and nipped. He wanted to gut the horses, but this was a decent job and so, resolved, he tried to be as normal as possible. He turned his gaze from the draught horses as the lead horse reared slightly, its left rein going taut as its hooves clapped on the stone.

The following evening, after the men had finished loading the beer, they got their weeks pay. Some of the men asked Elias to go to the corner bar with them. With apprehension he agreed. The place resounded with the sound of laughter and men trying to talk over one another. He didn't want to sit at the bar. He didn't like having his back to the entrance, but he said nothing to them. Instead, he bought a round of drinks and tried to act natural, tried to ignore the mirror's chattering, to be one of the guys. He crawled with anxiety though, the palms of his hands rubbing incessantly on the knees of his pants as the smell of smoke and beer and the sweat of men climbed then surrounded him.

He never noticed her. He never sensed her moving through the crowd, squeezing between the tables and the men and the servers with their trays and their dresses and their clanking empty glasses. It wasn't until she swept past him allowing her hair to swing and faintly brush across the back of his neck that he became aware.

The smell of flowers lingered, jasmine, he thought as he whirled around, but he couldn't place it. She was gone.

"Did you see a woman in here, Jacque?" Elias asked the man sitting next to him.

"No. Not one I'd take home to my mother, if that's what you mean."

With a smile, Elias turned back towards the bar and slid his hand into the handle of the mug of beer. "Maybe it was that ruddy server, Elizabeth?"

"She's working tonight," Jacque said grinning then tipping back his beer, "but I don't think I'd take her home to my mother either."

Chapter 5

It was the sound of the waitress, Jaime placing the bill on the table that roused Elias. Like a fool he'd nodded off and into the sordid nostalgia of his past, his hand still grasping the bottle as he looked up and opened his eyes. She was fuzzy. He smiled at her and then placed the empty bottle of bourbon to his lips and tipped it. He found nothing but emptiness inside. Nothing. Smiling again, he sat the bottle down and slid it wobbly over to her as she instinctively snatched it by the nape between her index and middle fingers.

"Is your lady friend coming back for you?" Jaime said as she collected the two glasses from the table.

"I don't need her," Elias huffed.

"You're sauced."

"I'm fine. I just need to hit the head."

"Well, if Lady in Red isn't back here in a few minutes to collect you I'm gonna call you a cab."

"You're a persistent woman, Jaime," he said, pushing his hand through his hair and then pulling his money clip out and flipping the bills and setting them on the check.

"You need change?"

"Keep it," he said, scooting out of his chair.

"Thank you, hun," she said. "You've got ten minutes then I'm calling the cab," she continued as she took the money from the table and walked towards the bar smirking.

Elias rubbed his eyes and drew in a breath of the smoky air and then turned and went towards the restroom. As he opened the door he was greeted by the mingled smell of lilac from a small white mechanical mister on the wall and stale urine. He tried to ignore it as he approached the urinal and as he cleared his thoughts he realized that the mirror had become unusually quiet, too quiet in fact. He let his head rest against the cool tile on the wall as he peed. He thought about the mirrors silence. He thought about what it might mean if the Katoptron had turned on him as he had turned on it and that it may understand what he meant to do. He focused entirely on it and in the silence he heard it calling. It escaped faint and light like a message on the wings of a butterfly, but he heard it, that lulling voice calling in the darkness, the chasm that existed between life and death. What disturbed him was the mirror was calling someone else.

Finishing, Elias went to the sink and washed his hands and pooled the water in his palms and washed the cool water over his face, his eyes and through his hair until his hair ran wet in thick black furrows. In the mirror on the wall a young man's face peered solemnly back at him. Elias looked at the unblemished skin, the façade that encased what he knew to be true. He watched the droplets of water run down his cheek and he touched, with quavering fingers, the spot where in the clutches of the Mississippi a branch had punctured through to his teeth and then so violently torn free. His

The Reflection of Elias Dumont

fingers grazed the skin, but there was no scar. There was only a memory, a phantom.

He shut the water off and left the restroom grabbing his cigarettes as he passed the table, tucking them into his pocket as he pushed on along the bar and out the door and into the humid air of the night. Outside, the streets lay relatively quiet. There was the occasional sound of a car passing somewhere in the distance and the dull hum of an air-conditioning unit. Elias stood on the side walk for a moment with his hands in his pockets and then he began to walk. He made it two blocks when a cab pulled up along the side of the road and the door swung open. There, in the backseat, sat Echo, her arm outstretched and a look of panic in her eyes.

"Get in," She said as the sound of a shotgun rang and the terrible burn of a slug tore into Elias's back then exploded from his chest. The wound made a sucking sound as the air escaped from the hole in his lung and as he turned he saw Videl and felt another slug tear through his shoulder, a puff of rusty powder bursting from the wound.

"I'd be careful with that thing," Elias choked, pulling his shirt up to expose the mirror tucked into the front of his pants. Material, powdered with the dust of his blood, fell as the shirt bunched and the mirror hissed with all its contempt for Elias.

"The Katoptron is mine, Dumont," Videl bellowed, his voice thick with a resonating bass. "It calls to me."

He saw Videl charge towards him, like a grisly Abe Lincoln necromanced from the grave, a tall black hat fixed upon the crown of his head, his trench coat flapping as he came and then Elias was in the cab, in Echo's arms, nestled in her lap as she held him and the cab sped away.

The cabby swore franticly and threatened to throw them both out of the cab, but neither of them was paying attention to him. Elias found himself where he had longed to be, in Echo's arms, but the dying was over and the wounds had closed and the nightmare continued. Had Videl shot him in the head, knocked him down then maybe things would have been different. And what if Videl had gotten the mirror back? What would have become of him then? The question and concern faded from him as the smell of jasmine filled his senses, as he breathed her in. He was delirious with it. There came a longing to be suffocated by it as his face pressed against her chest and Elias's ear took in the strong and virulent heart beat, a heartbeat he had not felt in his own body for over a hundred years. He felt alive as she held him and when he sat up there were tears in his eyes. The vinyl seat groaned as he sat back and let his head rest against the seat. Echo placed her hand in his and when she did Elias noticed how warm she felt. The heat radiated from the tips of her fingers.

"I saw you get shot," the cabby bellowed.

"Just pull off," Elias said, perturbed by the man's voice.

"I saw you get shot..."

"Just stop the damn cab."

"The bullets came out of your chest. I saw – "

And then the knife drove into his neck. The cabby made an awful gurgling noise as the blood raced from the artery, spraying the passenger side window and as Elias pulled the knife back out the cab plowed onto the side walk and over a meter and another and another until it curved off again and into the back of a parked Ford Tempo. The horn blared as Elias staggered from the car and onto the sidewalk. In the air the sweet smell of radiator fluid fumed from the wreck and as he righted himself he saw Echo in the car, leaning over the front bucket seat of the cab, her lips locked on the gushing wound of the cab drivers neck.

Seeing her there suckling the gash made him realize all the more that they were abominations, two things born into misery to scourge the earth. There lurked an urge in him to turn and run away, to leave her there in her blood feast as he had so many years ago. But, he knew the trance she was in. It was this type of fevered catch when she was most vulnerable, that enamored state as she lay visible to the world and her conscious became lost to the swoon and the rapture of the kill.

There was a man down the road jogging with a large dog and further down he saw the headlights of a car and so he went in and grabbed her by the wrist. "Come on," he said as he pulled. "There are people coming."

The lamia turned her head and hissed. Her eyes were wild and brilliant and in her mouth her fangs were exposed. They were not at all like teeth as he had supposed, but milky and opaque like the venomous fangs of a serpent. She looked like a cobra rearing to strike.

"Echo," he growled. "Get out of the cab."

With another hiss she lurched forward. Her skin was dark and rich and flushed and the man's blood was smeared about her lips and cheek. It was clear she was confused, unaware of whom he was or where she was and so Elias grabbed her and held her to him. He staggered with her in his arms down the side walk, felt her sink her fangs into the meat of his neck, felt her reel and then come off as he shuffled into an alley with a quickened step. She began to calm. The muscles in her back relaxed as her hands came unclamped from his shoulders and her arms slid around him. He held her tightly as he ran, her cheek coming to rest on his nape, the smell of her hair faint and pleasing as it jostled, the strands grazing his face. Elias wanted to keep her in his arms like this, but when they reached the next street she kissed him lightly at his temple and then slid out of his arms and onto her feet.

"You dumb bastard," she said grinning.

"What?"

"You nearly killed me twice tonight."

"Does that surprise you?" he shrugged. "It's what I do best."

"Stop your cynicism."

"I'm not being cynical I'm being honest," he said taking her hand as they walked, the moon waning in the sky as the sound of sirens whined far off in their rush towards the hopeless scene they'd left behind. "And what do you mean twice?"

"Well, the first was the risk you took of exposing me. I have no desire to be left out in the sun by a pack of mortals."

"Yes, I understand that."

"Do you," she scoffed. "Because, I don't think you do."

"I understand, it's just…" he said, stopping along the curb and looking down Forest Park Ave. and then at the cracks in the side walk, scuttling a small ant hill with the toe of his boot. "It's just, I can't help it."

"Of course you can."

"I can't. I've tried and I can't."

"But, you enjoy killing."

"No. I'm not like you. I saw you there in the cab in your throw of ecstasy. You would have stayed latched to him until every ounce of his blood had been let from his veins. You enjoy killing."

"I never said I didn't. Killing is sport for me. Killing excites me. Yes, killing is how I live and killing is how you live, Elias."

"But, I've never taken pleasure in it. It's never what I wanted. I don't want to kill them it just happens. I can't control it. It's the mirror, Echo, the mirror. Its voice is ever in my head."

He pulled the pack of cigarettes from his pocket and fidgeted with the lid to the box until it opened, then he gave her a cigarette and placed another in his own mouth striking the lighter, and cupping the flame with his hand and the pack of smokes as he brought it to her face. The light from the flame brought the color out of her skin as she leaned in and sucked and lit the smoke. Then he lit his own cigarette and placed the pack and the lighter back in his pocket and blew the smoke out into the dark purplish glow of the city sky where it was never truly dark for the lambency of modern civilization.

"You really do want to die, don't you?" she said, the smoke twisting upwards from her cigarette as her eyes softened to him.

He smoked and said nothing.

"I believe that if the sun could have killed you on the first day of your being born into this that you would have gone out that morning and embraced the sun as it rose to burn you away." She stepped closer to him again and took a drag from her smoke, watching the hurt wash over him. "What made you hate immortality so much?"

"I didn't always hate it," he snapped.

"No?" she said, as they began to walk east on Forest Park Ave. crossing North Grand Blvd. towards the hotel.

Along the left side of the boulevard were trees and for a moment Elias walked without saying anything else. He just walked and let the sound of the leaves in the wind calm him, their gentle rustling above the long expanse of concrete and black top that led back to the Mississippi, to the Arch and to the hotel where Robert lie dead in his room. With a deep breath he pitched his cigarette in the road and took Echo's hand. She grew happier when he did this, her fingers intertwining with his as they walked.

The Reflection of Elias Dumont

"I'm sorry I left you before," he said, "but I was afraid… well, I was… I was afraid I would destroy you if I stayed.

She said nothing as they walked now, only listening to Elias and the occasional car with its flapping tires on the cracks in the road and the warm rush of air as it passed them. She said nothing and the moon said nothing and the air was perfect as Elias opened to her, giving her what she had longed for. He spoke as he had never done. In all the long years that she had known him, he had never confided in her, never told of how he came to be this damned immortal. He told her of that day along the Mississippi when the earth shook and the river flowed backwards. They walked in the grass between Forest Park Blvd. and Grand Forest Drive, he telling her of how the fissure formed and how the great wall of water came and swallowed him, carrying him away as the murky water drowned him and the debris ripped at him until the black trunk came, that strange twist of fate, so it seemed, as his hand grasped the handle and his life took a new direction.

"I was eighteen," he said as they reached the intersection at South Compton.

"Funny, you look at least nineteen," she said as the light changed and they crossed, laughing as they walked until they reached the other side where Forest Park became Market.

"When I awoke the next morning," Elias continued, "I was laying next to the trunk and when I opened my eyes I found three Indians standing over me. One was poking me with a stick. His name was Ka'-wa-ska, which meant Black Horse, he told me as he offered me his hand and helped me to my feet. The other two, Hon'-ga and his sister Ha'-ba-tu, could not speak English only broken French, which I found was excessively limited as well.

Merci beaucoup, I told them, thank you as the girl came closer to me and held my arm, gesturing to the other two at my face where the limb had punctured through. She had me sit on the trunk and as she examined the wound I felt the oozing run down my cheek and into my throat. The taste and the feeling of it made me flush and vomit. Ha'-ba-tu then placed some type of mud on the wound, which Ka'-wa-ska said would help it to heal and then we placed the black trunk on a horse and strapped it down with leather straps.

After walking for a time I thanked Ka'-wa-ska again and asked him whose horse this was as there were four horses but only three riders. He proceeded to tell me that his brother, Mi'-da-in-ga or Playful Sun had been killed when the earth shook. I told him I was sorry for his loss and he nodded, keeping his chin firm and the reins of the horse drawn tight in his hands. He then explained what business they had in the region and that they were intent on trading pelts in New Madrid for ammunition and tobacco.

I told Ka'-wa-ska that my uncle, Francois, worked at the trading post and that I would make sure they were treated well for having helped me. The Indian nodded again with his stern face and pinched lips. Then he asked me how I came to be so far away from the town? I told him, I had been carried away by the river and that much of the ordeal was a blur, but the trunk had saved me as I floated atop it until the waters resided. That evening, when we stopped, we tied the horses to a tree that had fallen over and made our camp in a small clearing near the river. As we sat by the fire Ka'-wa-ska and Hon'-ga smoked a carved pipe and offered it to me and I thanked them, but declined as I did not smoke at the time and the pain in my cheek was exquisite.

As Ka'-wa-ska smoked and the fire crackled he told me that I had been touched by the spirit world and that perhaps it was his brother who had reached for me in the river and guided me to the trunk. He said my name in the Osage would be Non'-nun-ge, which meant Runner, for I had ran with the wild mighty river and survived. Merci beaucoup, I told him as he offered me the pipe again and in the cold still darkness I accepted. My body was shaking with the cold as I took the first pull from the pipe and pain burned in my cheek and then my lungs wrenched and coughed.

The two men patted my back and laughed as they passed the pipe around again and this went on until, in the black and starlit distance a rumbling was heard on the river that made the four of us stand dead silent with fear and then it came. It moved up the river in its defiance of nature, the giant wheel churning off the side of the vessel as it came sending the ripples of its wake ashore as we watched it pass. On the side of the steamboat were the words, New Orleans and as I went to yell and wave to the vessel Ka'-wa-ska grabbed my arm and bid me not to. As he did this I watched the bellows of black smoke belch from its stack into the gradients of darkness, of blues and grays and blacks that hosted the countless stars of that time, before the artificial light of this day diffused them.

I sat again as the cold bit my hands and listened to the wheel of the boat churn into the distance until all that was left was the sound of the water rolling ashore. The three Indians sat as well around the shrinking fire. None of them spoke. Instead, they sat and rocked in a meditative state as I went about looking for more wood to put on the fire. It wasn't until I returned and dropped the pile of sticks and logs on the ground that Ka'-wa-ska stirred.

When I asked him why he did not want me to signal the steamboat he said it was the steamboat that had been causing the disturbances on the river, that the boat was unnatural and that it angered the river and the earth. I told him I was certain it wasn't. I tried to explain that it was just a boat, but he had no intention of entertaining my ideas. Ka'-wa-ska then retrieved a copy of the Louisiana Gazette from a satchel that rested near his feet. It was rolled and crumpled and as I straightened it there were pages and strips missing, which, I surmised, were used as rudimentary toilet paper. As I'm sure you very well know this luxury was not yet prevalent in the America's. At least he wasn't using his left hand I thought as I smiled at him, the flames of the fire glowing red on his stoic face.

He made a gesture with his hand and then asked me if I would read a section of it to him and with a nod I agreed, scooting closer to the fire for the light, the embers crackling and hissing as I searched for the best angle in which to read and then, clearing my throat I began:

The Reflection of Elias Dumont

The comet which is now traversing our hemisphere may be seen every clear morning and evening. It rises about half past one in the morning and sets about half past 8 o'clock in the evening. Its present situation may be readily found by the cluster of stars, which are denominated the *Cleaver, Plough* or *Pointer*, near the north pole star. The elongation of a line from the *North* through the *South Pointer* will pass through or very nigh the *Comet*. Its appearance to the eye answers the description of Comets in the books, that of cloudy stars emitting a dull light and presenting no definite outline. Its present position as to the earth hinders its tail or blaze from being seen. The hair (coma) surrounds the nucleus (head) -- but projects upwards more in length than from any other part. Its *tail* is now seen lengthwise; should it be in a situation to be seen sidewise the full length of the blaze will be apparent: but it will appear of different lengths in different situations. It apparently is on its retreat from the *Sun* into regions of space -- and probably is the same seen some months since having passed its perihelion -- Anciently these sidereal erratics were held to be precursors of great calamities -- revolutions, pestilence and wars. But philosophers of later years have ascertained their nature to be like that of the planets "*parts of one harmonious whole.*" It is calculated there are about four hundred and fifty belonging to the solar system.

When I finished reading the article I looked at Ka'-wa-ska. He was gazing contemplatively towards the stars as the other two spoke to one another in Osage and so I looked up as well and thought about how the Ancients may have been right all along, precursors of great calamities I pondered. What could be worse than the calamity I had endured I wondered and then I rolled the gazette back up and tried to give it to Ka'-wa-ska, but he motioned for me to keep it.

"Merci bien," I told him as I went about re-stoking the fire and then I got up and turned and went to the horse where the trunk was sitting on the ground. The cold air was settling into my bones, causing my body to continuously shiver. It had occurred to me then that there may be some articles of clothing in the trunk to help keep me warm as I was freezing and surely would have suffered greatly through the night. Kneeling, I found there were two brass latches that folded forward, which kept the lid shut and a third clasp in the center for the use of a lock to secure the box.

I tell you, Echo, I felt fortunate when I knelt before the black trunk and found there was no lock upon it only the two brass latches, which I flipped open directly. Inside there were certainly clothes, several shirts, under-cloths and to my great satisfaction a pair of leather gloves and a scarf, but lying atop these garments was something I did not expect, but something that had expected me all along. What lay there, Echo, was the

The Reflection of Elias Dumont

Katoptron. It lie face down with the mirrored surface resting on the garments and the handle pointing towards me and I could hear its voice in my mind like the voice of my conscience, that inner voice of reason, but now it was there supplanting in its mystical way.

It was like I had fallen into a dream as I reached for the handle and when I picked it up I felt a great energy like static in the marrow of my bones and then I looked upon it as a blind man might look upon the world for the first time with all of its marvels. I let my fingers grace the carvings on the handle, touched the beautiful boy Narcissus and his reflective twin image and then I turned the mirror over.

At first there was nothing in the pane save an eerie blackness and then it locked my gaze so that I could not turn my face or overt my eyes. All my peripherals became blurred until the world around me fell into nonexistence. I felt helpless as I knelt there and then a face came into the mirror, but the face was not my own. This was a hideous face, distorted and grotesque. It wailed and groaned in a torturous manner as my tremulous hands held the Katoptron.

Then another face came, one even more frightening then the first. It was twisting and screaming in the darkness as its flesh decomposed, the rotting sinews tearing from its skeletal face as it reeled. I tried to scream out as the suffering demon coiled. But, I could not, the air was stolen from me, the words frozen on my tongue as one face came after another. With all my strength I tried to turn away, to simply blink, but I could not. Tears welled in my eyes as I thought I was going mad and then my face appeared. I sat gasping for a while. My body was tense as I placed the mirror in my lap and looked at my hands. The imprint from the flowers was there from the handle as I had been grasping the mirror so tightly. Then I heard her shudder."

"Did you kill her?" Echo pressed. "The Indian girl, was Ha'-ba-tu your first kill?"

"No," he said, eyes widening.

"But you did kill her."

"She started screaming and I was confused. I don't know, I guess part of me wanted to kill her, to quiet her and the mirror Echo, the mirror was coaxing me to do it. I remember lunging for her as she fell back, my hand clenching around her thin ankle as she fell to the ground. It was so cold. She seemed, so, fragile as I clawed my way atop her and then the other two were there. We struggled, our hot breathe vaporous as it left us and I became like a wild animal clawing, tearing at them until they held me down.

The mirror was furious. It burned in my mind as Ha'-ba-tu spoke in those unintelligible words and while I did not understand the language she spoke, I did understand her gestures, her body language, that it was clear something had happened to me or that I had done something wrong. She kept touching her face and shaking with her quivering finger pointing at me again.

I blurted obscenities at her, cruel things that I would have never spoken. It was as if I had no control of my body, my mouth or even my mind. I felt more like a spectator observing everything, even my own involuntary actions and the weeping girl as she clearly

The Reflection of Elias Dumont

gestured that I had attacked her and the two men's growing rage, their eyes dimmed, eyebrows pinched above their broad noses where their nostrils flared as their fists clenched and struck at me one after another. The pain was immensely fascinating. With each crushing blow I felt my flesh bruise and burn or split. I tasted the blood in my mouth again, felt them break my nose, but as each fist withdrew so did the pain until Hon'-ga leapt back with a look of horror on his face.

When Ka'-wa-ska saw this he attempted to get up, to move away from me as well, but as he stood up I grasped his wrist and with the other hand I clasped his knife and with a fluid motion pulled the blade from the sheath and him back down upon the blade. His eyes were wide with fear and death as he lay upon my chest. His expression was awful. It caused a shot of panic to rifle through me. I had never killed, let alone stabbed a man before and there I was face to face with this man who had shown me kindness, given me his brother's horse and I had repaid him with the murderous promise of the grave.

It was maddening. The panic I felt was wholly excruciating. His eyes fell into that questioning gaze, a look I have become all too familiar with, as the why's came pouring out of them like the warming blood that flowed from his wound and then it was done. I might have stayed there in that mortified state had the horses not began to rear and fit with agitation. Their hot breath plumed in the cold air as I rolled and slid the dead man from me and then I heard the cocking of a rifle. Hon'-ga had managed it from the pack on his horse and as I stood to face him he shot.

The sound of it rang loud and crisp in the cold dark air. I remember the deafening high-pitched tone that stayed in my ear as the echo of the shot trailed off. There was the wailing of the girl, Ha'-ba-tu as she stood with her knees and her stomach bent and her hands clasped over her ears and I stood there frozen with the blood of Ka'-wa-ska about me and a bullet hole in my stomach. There was the sound of the rifle clacking again, the bolt action as the Indian frantically reloaded and the mirror was saying, don't stop you fool they'll take it if you let them. But, the shock of everything was too much. I felt the hole in my gut with my finger, felt the blood oozing from the wound and then it closed. I was bewildered. The reality of it was incomprehensible and then the looking glass calmed me, its words saturating my mind as it whispered you are indestructible, Elias. You are indestructible.

A rush of power seized me as Ha'-ba-tu clumsily shot, the bullet whizzing past my ear as I charged him and before the smoke had cleared from the sulphurous air I brought the blade down upon him. It made a terrible gash from his forehead to his chin, the white fluid of his eye gushing out as he howled, as the rifle crashed to the ground and as he fell to his knees I realized I was laughing."

"You didn't kill her did you?" Echo interrupted.

"Kill her," Elias said, his eyes dimming as though the comment had drained his energy for a moment. "She was there, sobbing, frozen in some listless state of resign."

"And you," she said. "What of you?"

"I was in awe of myself. The implications of it, the knowing of it, Echo, that the mirror had made me immortal. It was like being born with all of life's knowledge. I dropped the knife to the ground and put my hands to my face. I felt the smoothness of my skin. It was like touching an angel and the looking glass whispered, yes. I looked at my hands, my perfect hands crusted with blood and I marveled at them and then I looked at the girl as she shivered and the tears ran down her cheeks, her hair in tangles.

I pitied her. And though I did not feel threatened the mirror urged me to finish this, to kill her, but I walked away, back to the trunk where the mirror lay atop the clothes and I picked it up and looked, the broken face staring back at me, the real me, the nose shifted, lips split, the jaw broken and there on the cheek a bloody hole. Again, my fingers ran across my face, feeling its smoothness and in the mirror the hand did the same, smearing the blood as it went. Then I lowered the looking glass to see the bullet wound, opening the hole in my shirt with my fingers and it was there in the reflection oozing red, but when I pressed my fingers to the wound I felt nothing but solid flesh. I stood horrifically amazed. Enthralled in the mystery of it, I tried to wrap my mind around what I had become. Good god, what had I become?"

Echo said nothing. She simply allowed her fingers to intertwine with his as the two of them crossed North Jefferson Ave. They walked slow as a dozen or more seagull's danced and squalled in the adjacent parking lot. Elias turned his head and looked at them, watched one ascend until it landed on a light post in the parking lot and when the two of them reached the other side of the avenue. They sat down on the round concrete retaining wall, watching the birds and the cars that passed and taking in the air, the breeze, the smell of the city. Behind them were small bushes that encircled an ATM machine and as he pulled another cigarette from its pack he noticed Echo running her long thin fingers across the needles of a bush.

He wanted to tell her again that he loved her. There were so many things he wished were different, so many things in his past that he would change if he could and as he lit the smoke she looked at him and smiled her luscious smile, teeth hidden, eyes gleaming with the electric light from above.

"Echo," he said, pushing his hand into his hair. "I wanted to tell you that I'm…"

"Do not apologize for the past," she interrupted, leaning towards him and taking the cigarette from his mouth. "Your eyes have done this a hundred times over. I know what lies inside you, Elias. I feel the guilt that you are stricken with. It poisons you as if it were lead in your veins." She took a long drag from the cigarette as she stood up and then she swung her hair over to one side, blowing the smoke into the night sky.

He caught the jasmine as she moved. It overpowered the must and exhaust of the street and he held on to it, like a firefly cupped in his hands he held it, savoring its fleeting existence before letting it go. "Will I see you tomorrow?"

"Yes," she said, running the back of her hand lightly down his arm. "I'll be waiting for you at the bridge over the River des Peres on Alabama Ave." With that she turned and began to walk back towards Forest Park.

"Echo," he said softly. "What was the other thing that almost killed you?"

With a pause she turned and tilted her head slightly allowing the long coils of hair to fall around her shoulder, "your dead blood," she said as her eyes closed slowly, her lashes delicate like the wings of a butterfly and then she turned and walked away.

Chapter 6

When Elias awoke the next afternoon, he was greeted by the sun and the faint smell of decay. He rolled over on his back, placing his arms behind his head and looked at the dead bellboy, Robert. For a moment, Elias studied him, studied how the sun illuminated his sunken features, his eyes protruding slightly from their sockets and he wondered if Robert had gone to heaven. Certainly, if there was such a place, Robert had gone there, but he was inclined to think that this was all there was, that we were born and lived and died and nothing more, that we had no soul and that the mirror was just something designed to cheat this, a window dressing of sorts that gave the perception of immortality, that even these so called immortals could be destroyed as he had surely destroyed many of them and that they were simply something within the realm of illusions and nothing more. He hated the thought of it.

With a scoff he turned on his side again and saw the mirror lying on the bed. The Katoptron was face up and above it he saw a myriad of dust particles floating aimlessly, each one like a fragment of silver as the sunlight glistened from its tiny surface. The mirror though, in its strange ways, did not reflect the light, but instead remained cold and dark and the particles nearest swirled as the light appeared to be drawn into it. It had the look of a small vortex, a miniature black hole bent on sucking the world into its oblivion. He hated the thought of this more and so he sat up, grabbed the handle of the looking glass and flipped it over.

The Reflection of Elias Dumont

The mirror offered a disturbing silence. Elias did not give it the satisfaction of his concerns though. Instead, he thought of the dream he had that night. It was a dream he'd had many years ago as well, a dream of him being hunted by a lion. In the dream the lion chased him through a dense brush, its brown mane flowing as it ran, as it charged closer until he could hear its panting and then it leapt and roared and tore him from his slumber.

"So, Robert," he said, leaning over the bed and pulling a clean pair of blue jeans and a black t-shirt from the trunk. "What were we talking about before?" he continued, laying the clothes on the bed and then bending again to retrieve a clean pair of socks and underwear. When he had them in hand he rose to his feet and picked the pants and shirt up then moved towards the bathroom. "You know, it's impolite to stare," he remarked as he stepped over the boy's legs. "I'll let you think on it then while I get a shower."

He'd nearly made it to the bathroom when he stopped and made an abrupt turn back towards the bed. "You thought I'd leave you alone with the mirror did you?" he chortled, snatching the looking glass from the bed and shaking his head. "I'm not that foolish." Then, with a complete disregard for the dead man, he marched into the bathroom, the door slamming behind him.

Elias was in the bathroom all of ten minutes and when he emerged he looked refreshed, his hair still wet and thick as it fell around his face. The black t-shirt clinging to his chest and back as he moved through the room for he had not properly toweled off and when he reached the bed he flopped gingerly down on the edge, lighting a cigarette as the water dripped from his head. With a flip, his hair went back then he adjusted the mirror so that it was more comfortably tucked in the front of his pants and went about placing his left foot on his right knee.

He sat like this until the cigarette burned three quarters gone, the long arched ash clinging in defiance to gravity and then he pointed it at Robert and said, "Alright then. I can see you are a persistent fellow. That is a quality," he continued, the ash falling in a small pile upon the gray carpet, "and I can tell you will not budge before you hear the end of this."

Elias placed the smoke in his mouth then, letting his hand come to rest around his ankle. "Well, you know of course I had to leave that place. New Madrid became problematic and besides I had a mission," he said, getting up again and moving to the table in the room. He crushed the cigarette with his thumb as he looked out the window. The sun decanted around him as he looked out and into the sky.

"I keep having a dream, Robert. And each time the dream begins the same." He turned then, inebriated with the thought of it as he sank into the blue chair. "It first came a week before that unfortunate wretch Ferro arrived. Every night the lion came. I would see it there, the vivid image of it lurking with its hungry eyes and flowing brown mane. In that great lion, that king of beasts was the infinite desire to hunt me down and destroy me. I could feel it. What I learned though, young man, was that the dream was more a blueprint to the future, to what was to come, an illustrious tell which always preceded the arrival of one of my predecessors.

The Reflection of Elias Dumont

As I mentioned before, when they are close, the previous holders of the mirror, I see them in my dreams and in the mirror as well, but the lion, Robert, the lion unnerves me. Such a vision came to me again last night as it has for the past several nights. But, the clarity of this dream was matched only by one other dream. It was a dream I had prior to the night I was to board a Spanish ship bound for Puerto Rico.

The Port of Greater Baton Rouge, in 1817 had only just been incorporated. For two months I had lived there working the docks, loading and unloading freight, much of which was for the US Military, who, at this particular station, was under the dutiful eye of Brigadier General Daniel Bissell of the Army's First Infantry. Now I can tell you that Bissell was a man of honor, a man who had valiantly led his men during the war of 1812 and was most notably recognized for efforts at the battle of Cook's Mill. It's important to mention this for, I, to the contrary, had been engaging in every sort of debauchery. It's when I took a liking to bourbon, which, by the way, I could certainly use a nip of right now.

Grinning, Elias sprung from the chair and over to the phone beside the bed, pressed zero for the front desk and was greeted by the pleasant voice of a woman. "Hotel services, how may I help you?"

"Yes, hello, I was wondering if I could get some things delivered to my room."

"Of course," the woman said. "Will hold for a moment?"

"Certainly."

He heard the woman place her hand over the receiver and then he listened to her give muted directions to a man inquiring about a laundry room. "I'm sorry for that," the voice intoned with a smile, "and what would you like, sir?"

"Well, I would like two bottles of bourbon."

"Two bottles, sir?"

"Yes."

There was a pause and then she cleared her throat. "Any particular brand?"

"Wild Turkey, if you have it. If not, surprise me."

"Wild Turkey or similar," she repeated back, "and would you like anything else, sir?" she asked, her amenity resonating on the line.

"Yes, a bucket of ice please, a couple packs of Lucky Strikes and could you have that restaurant downstairs prepare me a steak, medium well?"

"I see there are instructions to leave such things on a cart outside your door. Is this correct, Mr. Bingham?"

"Yes, please. I do not wish to be disturbed. Just have the charges and the tip added into my bill and

The Reflection of Elias Dumont

when it is delivered have them knock once on the door. I will come to get it when I am ready."

"And you said you wanted this charged to your room," she said reflexively, the keys of her computer clacking into the phone. "Is there anything else then, sir?"

"No, thank you," he said, hanging the phone up and returning to the chair. "Bingham," he said aloud. He hadn't thought of the name since he checked in. It took him all of a second to forget the name again as he looked at Robert and shrugged it away. "Now what were we talking about? Oh, yes, yes my dream."

Pulling his knife from the sheath, Elias looked at his pale reflection in the dull silver blade. He turned the handle slowly as he spoke watching the image reappear with each rotation. It caused his mind to drift until the face became, not his, but that of the second lion come to call, the second of those seeking the mirror once more and, coincidentally, the second to have possessed the looking glass in the first place.

"The dream," he said, eyes fixed on the image in the blade, "was that of a Roman, a man named Licinius Cassius Sabaco." As the name rolled from Elias's tongue he made a swift flick with his wrist. The motion sent the large knife cutting through the room until it struck with a thud in the dry wall just above Robert's head. "He was a clever bastard, my friend and he damn near got the mirror from me. I believe my dispatching of William Ferro had made me overconfident, that and the utter vanity that the looking glass brought out of me, its constant reassurance that I was somehow greater than any who had preceded me and certainly better than anything the future had to produce.

Licinius was a terrible brut though, cunning and trained in the art of war. This was knowledge I attained in a dismal manner. Now, as I was describing a few minutes before, my drinking and consorting with loose women had risen to new heights and this in concert with my foolish vanity placed me in the frightful situation of nearly losing the Katoptron or worse. I had taken to running with some free spirited Cajun's and we often took to drinking heavily at a popular brothel in town.

Behind this brothel was a scattering of cypress trees and one in this bunch was especially tall with its base fanning out and a fine layer of moss that covered the bark. At its foot was a number of large stones and it was here that I would hide the looking glass while I engaged in these heathenish activities. And I know this sounds foolish and wildly dangerous, but at the time I found it logically less dangerous than leaving the mirror exposed while I lay equally exposed with a woman, a woman that could easily stumble upon the mirror or one who perhaps may have the idea to rifle through my clothing and rob me as I lie sleeping in that inebriated state of bliss and exhaustion.

It was, in fact, a very similar state of indiscretion, on the evening of that dream, that I was pulled away from the loving bosom of such a woman by four infantry men, who in their own drunken state, were quite agitated, accusatory and deplorably foul tongued. These men in their misguided manhandling of me took me into the street where they drew their swords upon me and were determined to disembowel me over my alleged thievery. I had no desire to scuffle with them. Their swords were not my concern either. What worried me more was the revelation to these men that their swords would have no lasting effect on me and that their attempts to cut me down in the street would only lead to their own dumfounded deaths, a scene that could be witnessed by any passerby or ogler from a window.

It happened as I stood there though, with the infantry men prodding me, that I noticed him approaching. He came at a steady pace and I knew at once that it was Licinius Cassius Sabaco for when I saw him I felt the breath of the lion upon my neck and I shuddered. He had my clothes in his hands and as he approached I could see the deep nasolabial folds that carved their way around his mouth. He looked like a hell-born Sharpay. The folds of skin on his cheeks and forehead were riddled with scars and there below his scowl was the grisly empty socket that once housed his left eye.

I thought of that eye, how he had lost it and the mirror in one fantastic volley of arrows, a volley that simultaneously transformed him from a, would be god, and into a tragic figure felled in a battle lost forever from the history of man. The scars besmirched him far deeper than the skin revealed. It was as if the word insignificant had been pierced into his face that night, as the Roman Legionaries were massacred around him, their weapons claimed as spoils of war and the looking glass lifted from the leather strap that secured it against his chest, lifted by a cloaked figure who moved upon him like a shadow and then disappeared. How ill he must have felt when he came to and found the mirror was gone, his body littered with Carthaginian arrows and that shaft he had to pull from his blinding wound, the wound that rendered him unconscious but for a few precious minutes.

When he reached me I stood tall and he grunted out my name, Dumont, as he threw my clothes at my feet. I imagine I must have appeared to the others like some heroic nude out of a classical painting. Licinius made no notice of it though. He just glared with his piercing black eye and then I detected a faint grin as he turned to the other men and thanked them, with his monotone voice, for capturing the thief that stole his mistress's mirror.

"So where is it, thief?" he said, pointing his eye back at me.

"I don't know what you're talking about," I told him. "I am no thief."

As I said this one of the men pressed the point of his sword into my throat and as it pierced slightly I noticed the Roman's face turn red, saw him slide his sword from its sheath and saw the anger in his eye grow wild as if I were the man who had lifted the mirror from him on the blood soaked field. "You'll tell me where it

The Reflection of Elias Dumont

is," he bellowed "or I'll cut you to ribbons and feed you to the bloody fish."

I was quite prepared at this moment to either attack the four men and surrender one of their swords, which would have resulted in many a laceration about my body or perhaps use a method of shocking my adversaries by impaling myself on the man's sword and likely taking a gut shot from Licinius's wide gladius, a sword he had undoubtedly wielded for centuries and then stepping away to show the four infantry men that I was not only happily alive, but healing before their eyes. It was as I deliberated in my mind that there came a sudden voice of command above the ruckus of the men. To my great satisfaction it was the clarion voice of Brigadier General Daniel Bissell, who on his way back to his quarters had, to my great fortunance, witnessed my frightful state and immediately saw fit to end this public indecency.

"Good god," Bissell sounded. "What's the meaning of this?"

The four soldiers immediately lowered their swords and snapped to attention as the General stepped between us. Licinius's chest heaved with each fuming breath, his hand still clenching the handle of his sword tightly.

"Speak up," Bissell said. "I need someone to tell me why in the hell four of my men are interrogating a naked man in the middle of the street?"

Shaking, one of the men, who appeared to be the youngest of them, blurted out, "it was the Dragoon, sir. He said this man had stolen something from his mistress."

"Gravois is this true?" the General asked, turning towards me.

I had assumed the name Bernard Gravois when I arrived as I had relieved a gentleman of said name from his credentials, purse and ensuing life, this taking place on my flight south. Now after arriving from New Madrid and going to work on the docks, I came to be in the company of the good General on several occasions for many an item was often shipped to his attention and I, being a young man with a likable face, was charged with delivering these items to Daniel Bissell myself. There for it was this name that he knew me by and on more than one occasion he had stopped me and talked to me of my potential and that I certainly would make a fine soldier if I were so inclined.

Of course I had given him a deaf ear on the subject, but this short history between us was enough to lift me out of my dire situation. "No, sir," I answered, pulling my pants up and buttoning them.

"He's lying, General," Licinius growled, "and his name is not Gravois it's Dumont, Elias Dumont."

"Well, I believe you are mistaken Dragoon," Bissell demanded. "I know this young man personally."

The Reflection of Elias Dumont

"You think you know him, but he is a liar, a thief and a killer."

"A killer! Do you know this man, Bernard?

"I've never met this man before in my life, sir," I insisted. "I would swear it on the Bible."

Taking notice of the General's disbelief of the accusations, the Roman realized that his plan had unraveled. To my surprise, a calm washed over him as he slid his sword into its sheath, but the eye remained wild with fury and contempt. "Perhaps the spirits have gotten the best of us tonight, General."

"Yes, I believe they have."

With that, Licinius Cassius Sabaco nodded, turned and began to walk away. I was buttoning my shirt as he did this and before he made it three steps away I noticed he had my knife tucked into the back of his belt. "Excuse me, sir," I called, "but, I believe you have my knife."

The other men looked at him when I said this and he stopped, shifting his head to one side, but he did not turn around, he did not breathe a word, he simply stopped and stood beneath the poor light of the whale fat street lamp. When it was clear he was not going to turn around, I looked at the General who was standing with his arms crossed and his eyes narrowed and then I looked at the men who were baffled by his behavior, the youngest one shrugging his shoulders in that questioning way and then I proceeded to walk cautiously towards the silent figure. As I did this he turned slowly around and slid the knife out from behind his back. He was emotionless. I had never seen a man so in control of his faculties and when I reached him he held the knife out for me to take it.

"My apologies," he said as he placed the knife into my hand, his eye dark and cold with just a sliver of light across the pupil.

"Thank you," I said and then I heard him speak, but it was not Licinius's voice, but the voice of the looking glass. It came clear in my mind as my eyes locked on his eye in some dark communion, his mouth shut with a slight grin barely noticeable between the folds on his cheeks and the voice said "I will find you Dumont and I will make you suffer for this." Then he nodded again and turned and walked away."

A single knock came then at the door of Elias's room. He stood up and walked with a cat like prowess across the room to the foyer and he listened, with his ear just a fraction from the door. Outside the door he heard the voices of two women. The one was just starting her shift, as she had gotten to work late and she stood talking to the other who had delivered the cart and they were laughing and then the one who had delivered the cart bumped the cart as she moved past it and they fell into laughter again. Elias gave them a few minutes then he walked across the room again to the corner where a door led to the adjoining room and he slid the key card to unlock the door then he opened it and walked into the next room where the door on that side had been left open.

    For many years he had used such decoy rooms as he felt they offered him more security and a means of escape if need be. One can never be too careful he thought as he moved through the room to the door and when he opened the door he peered outside and looked around. There was nothing in the hall save the cart. He could see the bourbon and he smiled as he stepped into the hall and so he let the door close as he moved towards the cart, but as he did this a man came around the corner and began to walk towards him. Instinctively, Elias reached for his knife as a burst of panic entered his mind. The man was getting ever closer as they both walked towards one another and to Elias's mortification he found his sheath empty. He had left the knife stuck in the wall inside the room and thus had left himself defenseless.

    His paranoia was terrible and unfounded. To his great relief the man stopped and turned towards the door adjacent from his room just as Elias reached the cart and then the man looked at him and said hello. Elias smiled and nodded then went inside his room with the cart. He could smell the steak. If it was like the one he had the previous night it would be a large cut, an inch thick, sweet with the juices of the fat and lightly covered in seasonings. He could taste it just as he could taste the bourbon and as the door closed behind him he let go of the cart and turned and brought the lever over, locking the door and then he turned to Robert.

"This may be my last meal, my friend," he said, grasping the handle of the knife and working it back and forth until it came out of the wall. It left a patch of white drywall powder on the dead bellboy's hair. "But, that's of no consequence to you," he continued, sliding the knife into its sheath and then returning to the cart. He picked a bottle of bourbon up first. They had delivered two bottles of Bushmills White Label whiskey and it satisfied him greatly. The sound of the glass bottle tinged on the metal cart as he sat it back down and then he pushed the cart across the room to the table where the sun was still incredible and he sat down with the light washing over him and moved the plate to the table, removing the lid and placing his nose over the steak to smell its sweet aroma. His eyes closed briefly as he did this and then he smiled and sat the lid on the tray in exchange for the Irish Whiskey, its seal popping as he turned the cap and when it was off he sat the cap on the table and took a couple of good whiffs before setting the bottle on the table as well. It was certainly different than any Tennessee bourbon but a pleasant surprise he thought as he placed the cubes of ice into a glass then poured the straw colored liquor in and drank it down. Replacing the whiskey immediately, Elias rested the glass and bottle on the table.

"So, Robert," he said, cutting into the steak and forking a piece into his mouth. "As I was telling you before, Licinius had walked off and the general had lectured his men and I on the pitfalls of over indulgence and after swearing to him that I would stay clear of the Dragoon, for he and his ilk were of a seedy and loathsome repute, as dreadful as any mercenary or the

The Reflection of Elias Dumont

like, I went promptly back to the brothel where my friends were still engaged in the merriment of the atmosphere, finding easily the room of my lady friend so that I may reacquire my boots. She of course put on a splendid guise of concern for my well being, which was to the utter indignation of a man she had so quickly exchanged me for.

I told her it was nothing as I picked the boots up from the floor then I nodded to the gentleman and graciously left the room, closing the door behind me. Ah, the look on that man's face was something," Elias laughed as he chewed the meat. His long sun-struck eyes gazed out of the window, lost in thought as he drank the glass of whiskey and then turning again he forked another piece of steak into his mouth.

"You know that bastard was waiting for me when I went back for the mirror," he continued, waving the steak knife towards the dead-man as he spoke. "When I left the brothel I thought I had sufficiently circled around, staying out of sight as I entered the woods and came through the cluster of cypress trees. You could imagine how I felt when I knelt down, pulling the stone away and lifting up the mirror only to hear his stoic voice. The sound of him struck me like a bolt from Zeus. It made my stomach leap into my throat and I swallowed coarsely as I stood to face him, tucking the looking glass into the front of my pants as he advanced, drawing his gladius as he came.

His first thrust nearly impaled me and I still don't know how I managed to avoid it. I remember falling sideways as I moved, my knees coming down on the stones at the base of the tree. The second slash came across my face and at first I thought it had missed me as well until I saw my nose lying in my lap. A pitiful moan escaped me as I looked and then another thrust came, but I rolled and the sword plunged into the sod and the nose was lost. I scrambled then to get to my feet, to run from him and he chided me as I did this. He called me a coward, Robert. What was I to do though? After all, I was yet a young man, inexperienced in the art of swordplay and he a professional killer, schooled in the brutalities of the Roman Empire, honed in the trudges of war.

    Self preservation is what had me run. I ran with him chasing, with his lion breath at my winged heals. I ran through those dimly lit streets, the sound of his feet falling further away as I pressed and my lungs heaved. This went on until I could run no more, but I lost him. I lost him in the streets, in the shadows I had become accustomed to. My lungs felt as if they were afire when I stopped, my teeth floating in my mouth as I choked in the air. It caused me to vomit, that or my nerves and when I finished with the heaving I collected my wits and placed my hand to my nose to feel the thing that was there and there was a nose, but I knew, I knew the terrible truth.

    It was a very long time before I looked into the mirror again, perhaps several years. I know it was a very long time though and when I did look again and saw my smitten face I wept and swore to that image that I would exact an awful revenge. Surprisingly, I did not meet up with Licinius for another five years. I think this was mostly due to my transient behavior, for once I left that sweet Port of Baton Rouge I fell in love with the sea."

Chapter 7

Placing his hand in the bucket of ice, Elias withdrew two more cubes and placed them in his glass, then he filled the glass half full with the amber colored whiskey, swirling it as he reclined into the blue chair. There was still a large portion of the steak left on his plate, but the bourbon was beginning to hold precedence over him and the sun had moved in its westerly habit allowing the room to calm with an easier light. Outside, he watched the river again, the Mighty Mississippi, as it swelled and lapped at the feet of the Gateway Arch. Beyond it he could see the stranded river boats with their gangways submerged and before them just the tops of the street lights stuck out of the muddy water. The name Non'-nun-ge floated through his mind as Elias drank. "And still we run," he whispered as the ice shifted and clinked in the empty glass, "still we run."

Turning his head away from the window again, he placed the glass on the table and proceeded to take a long guzzle from the square bottle. "I left Baton Rouge, my friend," he continued, wiping his mouth with the back of his hand, "aboard the Spanish ship *The Pride*, which on its mast carried the flag of Mexico, a delightful ruse, for the ship was captained by the pirate Jean Lafitte and so upon boarding her I was taken to the captains quarters where I was properly introduced to him as Bernard Gravois and he requested of me my oath of loyalty to him. I, of course, gave him this whole heartedly and soon we were underway in those intemperate waters of the gulf.

The Reflection of Elias Dumont

It was an exciting first journey for me and I acclimated to sea life exceptionally fast, to the great satisfaction of my fellow mates. I worked hard, rest assured, but in the evenings when the sun was setting I would watch the ocean roll like a vast seething skin, breathing in the salty air while the flying fish leapt in their precarious way, darting from a roll or a wave with a spray of water trailing behind them. Occasionally, one or two of them would land on the deck of the ship with their glistening skin and their gasping mouths or be snatched from the air by a bird. Hours passed in this manner. Often there were spinner dolphins about as well, racing with the ship as it sailed. They were an immensely playful lot and it was something to see their sleek gray body's bullet from the water and spin then cut back in again.

It wasn't until we had been out to sea for a week that the true nature of our voyage was divulged to me. That's not to say that I was unaware of the ship having falsified documents for its journey, as the Captain had confided in me to an extent and had warned me of perils involved in the ships enterprises, but the specifics, my friend, the specifics were what I was lacking. We were sailing off the Eastern coast of Cuba when the Boatswain, Ignazio Vargaz, approached me. He had a sour look about him generally and a sour smell also, which was not uncommon aboard the ship. Men were not exactly hygienic in those days and Ignazio was an excessively sweaty man.

When he approached me that afternoon he asked, "Do you know how to handle that blade hanging from your belt?"

"What is there to know?" I told him.

"There are many ways to kill a man muchacho," he smiled, "and one cannot rely on luck with a blade." He then proceeded to pull a small knife from his boot and with the carved bone handle grasped in his palm and the blade held close to the outside of his arm he told me to come at him with my knife.

This troubled me, for often the mirror took hold of me and bade me to kill with a perverse nature and so I trembled slightly as I drew the blade from its sheath. How would I explain killing the Boatswain, I thought. But then he motioned his hand to come at him and I, with a thrust forward, was caught by him as he moved around, grabbing my wrist with his open hand and pressing the blade of his knife to my jugular. We repeated this time and time again and each time his blade found another vital area, another place to slip its lethal edge and I learned from Ignazio as the mirror persisted in its ways of corrupting my thoughts and bending my will and then I cut him.

The cut, however, was minor for he was nimble as a gazelle with the knife passing by him as his body arched and when he saw that I had grazed him he lifted his knife into the air and laughed, "Si, muchacho. You are getting the hang of it."

There was some laughter and shouting from a few of the crewmen who had gathered when he did this and he turned to them with an agreeable look and then he came to me and placed his hand on my shoulder. He was fully unaware of the battle raging in my head to regain control and I was terrified that my knife may at any moment lash out and finish what the looking glass so desperately wanted. It wanted him dead. It needed him dead, with his blood spilling on the wood decking of *The Pride*, but I knew if this happened I would have to kill every man aboard this ship or certainly be found out. As I thought of this the mirror conceded, slithering back into that dark region of silent anticipation, a place where the serpent lies coiled and reared and patient to strike.

"Are you alright, Ignazio?" I asked him as I slid the knife into the sheath. "I am sorry for cutting you."

"No, no," he said smiling. "I am fine."

"I must have gotten over zealous," I told him, pulling my handkerchief from my pocket and handing it to him.

He patted my shoulder again as he pressed the handkerchief to the slice just below his ribs then he gave me a serious look and said, "Come, Bernard. I have something to tell you." And so I followed across the deck and down the latter until we reached his quarters. It was a small cramped space with a single thin cot and as I watched him open a box and dig around he asked me to please sit. I was obliged by his hospitality despite the mirrors grumblings and so I sat at the edge of his cot with my feet pressed to the floor and with an exclamation of joy he produced two small cigars. It was strange to see him like this as he smelled one of the cigars and the sourness of his face melted away and then he offered me the other with a tip of his head and a raise of his brow and I naturally accepted.

Ignazio then educated me on the type of tobacco the cigars were made from, a mild leaf, he explained, from the fields of Virginia. He explained that the plant had many medicinal purposes as he wet the end with his lips and then he struck a match with the nail of his thumb and it popped and hissed as it erupted into flame. We each lit our cigars from it and then he dropped it on the floor and placed his boot over it as the toe ground it out.

"You are a man of potential," he said, the cigar gripped between his teeth. "That is why I want to tell you what is in store for us."

"Are we not going to Puerto Rico, Ignazio?" I asked

"No, hombre," he said smiling again. "We will be going to Puerto Rico, but it will be after we have acquired a certain cargo." Ignazio said this as he sat down upon a small wooden stool then he took a long pull from his cigar and let the smoke drift from his lips as he savored it. "There is a ship that we will be intercepting before we reach the white shores of Puerto

Rico. It is a ship filled with an unfortunate cargo, for it is a slave ship muchacho."

I nodded as he said this, for I was familiar with the slave trade, its many evils and the deplorable auctioning of those humans. Capital by the head they were, like any other commodity. "But the U.S. is moving to band the slave trade," I said. "I read it in the Gazette."

"Si, Bernard, but the Captain is a cunning man who understands the politics of this business. He has created letters of marque, from a nation of his design, that give his ships permission to attack any vessel it deems fit to seize."

"And we are to commandeer a slave ship then."

"Si."

"And then what?"

"We will sail it into Puerto Rico, where there are supplies awaiting us and then we will sail from there to New Orleans, where the negros will be offloaded and sold and once this deed is done we will sail to the island of Galveston."

"Galveston?"

"Si. It is an island off the coast of Texas. Captain Lafitte has taken control of this fort and established a colony there around Maison Rouge, the headquarters of our operations. It's what we like to call home," he said as his eyebrows rose slightly and a clump of ash fell from his cigar to the scuffed floorboards. "Do you think you are up to the task, this way of life, of pirating, muchacho?"

"Yes," I told him with a stern look and a slight nod.

Ignazio laughed and shook his head. "Good, good. Then there is an abundance of wealth in store for you. But beware, my young new friend, this is an ugly profession. This wealth comes in the payment of blood and a slave ship is a retched place.

Two days later we were on the weather deck when the lookout called that he had spotted a slaver North East of our position. Lafitte brought the ship into her course as the men readied their swords and knives, while others manned the swivel cannons mounted on the rails of the ship. Our sloop approached flying the Mexican flag at her masthead. As the sloop drew closer, they saw that she was armed with eight guns on her main deck and ten swivel cannons mounted along the rails, which the men had readied with grape shot, no less than forty pirates with the thirst and the thrill in their hearts, all waiting for their pirate captain, Jean Lafitte, to give the word.

The Slaver Captain, Jonathan Bicksbey, set more sail and endeavored to escape, but the wind was with us and the merchant ship, which sailed heavily laden, was no match for the faster sloop. *The Pride* gained on her

The Reflection of Elias Dumont

steadily and when in range began firing her guns. At eight o'clock by the setting sun we pirates came alongside and the chase was done.

What happened next was a nightmare for Bicksbey and his crew. We set about securing the slaver with our hooks and ropes and worked fast to board her. Two of our men were lost to pistol fire, but this only increased the brutality of those pirates who placed their boots upon that dour deck. The butchering was fierce with our Cutlass swords, boarding axes and our knives opening the gullets of those who resisted. My blade was especially cruel as the looking glass fell into a bloodlust and I was lost to the savagery of the moment. I remember sending the bodies over the side, into the rolling dark blue of the sea as the white caps broke and the sharks circled in their frenzy.

I watched several of the monstrous beasts break the surface with their great jaws open and their rows of teeth bore to take apart those frightful souls in the water. I shall never forget the sound of the sharks fins and tails and their great hulking masses roiling and turning in the water as the flesh and the bones of those men were loosed from their bodies. Two men from the slaver, Allen Landford, the ship's surgeon, who was twenty-two, and the first mate, Tanner Goldsmith, Thirty-four, were tortured as Ignazio ordered several men to bind them by the feet and lower them over the side where the sharks fed in that blood bath. They forced this upon the two men until they revealed the whereabouts of the gold stored onboard the ship. It did not take them long to forfeit this information. We were soon in the possession of twenty-four ounces of Spanish gold doubloon, and proceeded to ransack the rest of the vessel. We seized their pistols, gunpowder, the gunner's stores and the bosun's stores as well. We also removed two quarterdeck guns and two swivel guns and sent them across to our sloop, but the real haul for Lafitte, my friend, was the three hundred thirty-six males and two hundred twenty-six females, making in all five hundred sixty-two negros valued at £500 a head. The two men, Landford and Goldsmith, were then forced to join our lot of privateers. Two other of their mates joined us also, this of their own accord by freely swearing an oath to Lafitte.

    Having successfully commandeered the slaver, we set sail for the Eastern Port of Fajardo, Puerto Rico. It was something to watch the sun set that evening, its oranges and reds blazing across the water like fire and blood and I watched it from the helm as it burned and fizzled under, with Hector Vega, a salty dog from *The Pride*, who had commanded several of his own vessels and now he was teaching me how to navigate the seas. He drew a brass double achromatic telescope from a mahogany case and handed it to me and I looked through it at the heavens as Hector described the stars and their relationship to our course and heading and I absorbed every word that he spoke. There was a warm wind that rushed through my hair. I had the blue-black night with its endless stars stretched out before me. And I had the constant sound of the waves with my hands firm to the wheel and there I felt mightier than the Atlantic, than anything on earth. I felt god like and the mirror whispered yes, yes, yes.

The Reflection of Elias Dumont

We stayed two days in Fajardo, most of which was spent drinking heavily on the beach. Then, as Ignazio had said, we set sail for New Orleans. When we reached the port we had thrown overboard fifty-five negros, sending them to the giant sharks that followed our ships. The unfortunates were all enclosed under grated hatchways between the decks. The spaces were so low that they sat between one another's legs and subsequently were packed so near together that it removed all possibility of their lying down in any fashion or even changing their retched positions. Also, each negro was owned by or shipped on account of different individuals; this meaning that each was branded like common cattle with the owner's marks upon their flesh. These marks were branded onto their chests or onto their arms with a red-hot iron. It was a ghastly thing to behold as the negros were offloaded and sent into that unconscionable state of bondage and servitude.

I was relieved when we left that business behind and sailed for Galveston Island. Somehow killing a man was easier than subjugating them. I felt my life spiraling further into a darkness from which I could not return. I had lost so much already and now I was losing pieces of the very things that defined me, my ideals, the few that I had and so the desire to live began to wane. What was immortality if I couldn't enjoy it, if I couldn't tolerate what was happening around me, if I couldn't tolerate myself?

I suffered in this depression for more than a year until one evening Ignazio entered my berthing area to ask me a question. Upon entering he found I had succumbed to the ill pleasures of drinking rum and there, as I lay in the small bunk, he noticed a certain handle sticking out of my disheveled shirt. Curious of it he tried to reach it. As he did this the looking glass hissed and started me from that awful stupor. It caused my friend to jump back.

"Lo siento, Bernard," he said with his eyes wide and his body tense. "I only meant to trouble you for some tobacco."

"Of course," I said, but he was lying and I didn't need the mirror to tell me that he was lying, I knew. "It's there in the chest," I pointed, tucking my shirt back in over the Katoptron.

"Si," he said, with a bit of relief in his voice and then he smiled his sour looking smile for Ignazio always appeared to be stricken with an intestinal malady. Then he made his way to the chest.

"It's in the leather pouch there in the corner."

"Ah, very good," he said withdrawing the pouch and closing the lid of the chest and clasping the brass latches as he stood up and then he turned and asked if I would join him.

"Of course," I answered, rubbing my eyes with the palms of my hands as the desire to kill him boiled in me, but this was a man I had grown to love like a

The Reflection of Elias Dumont

brother, a man who had taught me so much and so I fought the urge.

That night we stood on the dock and smoked with several of the other crewmen and we laughed and drank and practiced throwing our knives into an old oak cask. I threw my blade over and over again in the manner Ignazio had taught me, pushing the hate somewhere deep below the surface, ignoring the voice inside my head and in the morning we rose and set sail. It was four days of choppy seas and gray skies with a rain that never really went away, but merely changed the degree in which it decided to come down. On the fifth day there was no rain, but the wind was strong and the waves crashed hard against the bow as the sloop's sails jibbed wildly and I worked to secure the riggings with the vessel dipping and rising with the waves. It happened on this day that a slaver was spotted.

The slave ship was bearing west and cutting across our course, but it was a considerable distance away. I could scarcely make it in the gray. It was more a silhouette in the distance as we plowed towards it, towards that ominous future and as the wind tangled and threw my hair about a coldness swept over me like the spray of the ocean.

It was dusk when we reached the slaver and as we came about her starboard side we exchanged cannon fire, for the slaver carried three thirty pound cannon on her quarterdeck. It was a devastating first volley for both sides as we sustained damage to our riggings due to their use of bar and chain shot. The shot also mutilated one of our crew as it tore and splintered across our deck. *The Pride* soon gained the upper hand though as we brought the slaver's mainsail down and pounded their deck with grapeshot. I remember Ignazio calling to me as we prepared to board the ship and I went to him and he placed his hand on my shoulder, as he always did and then the ropes and hooks went over as the cannon continued to fire.

The slaver was much larger than our ship and as we climbed her the sea heaved and swelled and the wind whipped at us while their crew fired blunderbusses loaded with clusters of pistol balls, shards of metal, nails and broken glass. We lost another five men before we reached the deck. Their casualties were not light either though for the crew manning our swivel cannon had continued to assault them with one blast striking just above me. I was covered in splinters of wood when I reached the rail and stepped over into the smoke and the bellowing of injured men as they lay on the deck, some of them badly mutilated or missing limbs. One of our crew sat against the bloodied deck, his back resting against the rail as his hands held his intestines. The man had the question in his eyes and the world seemed to be in slow motion again with the clash of swords and boarding axes around me and I looked at the gash along his abdomen and the intestines like a great serpent being born from him and then I looked at his eyes again as the life in them dimmed and the questions flooded them, the why's and the what if's and then I felt the smallsword go into my back and through and out of my stomach.

The Reflection of Elias Dumont

It was a strange thing to see the point of the blade sticking out of me and as the sword withdrew I had the taste of a coin in my mouth, but the blade had also dislodged the looking glass which I saw, in that same slow motion, fall from my pants with the handle going end over end until it struck the deck and tumbled once before coming to rest face up with all its darkness exposed to the world.

Immediately, I reached for it, dropping to my knees and then the sword pierced my back once more, but this time it tore through my ribs, my heart and I coughed a patch of blood upon the mirror. Again there came the metallic taste as I swallowed my own blood and then I felt the boot on my back and the blade wrenching out and I fell stunned beside the dark and silent mirror. It was like seeing my soul lying beside me. To my utter horror I saw Ignazio squat down and he said something to me that I could not make out and in his hand was the handkerchief I had given him and he wiped my blood from his sword, tossing it at me when he was through and then he picked the looking glass up and smiled.

When his hand touched it I felt a wrenching pain. It caused me to knot up and I believe I wailed as the reality of the situation gripped me, my hands pressed to my face, my fingers touching the dreaded hole in my cheek and the hollow where my nose once was. It frightened me like nothing before. But, Ignazio had not planned his betrayal of me well for as he beheld the Katoptron I began to rise with the fierceness of the lion I had dreamt of so often. He was mesmerized by the looking glass and unaware of his surroundings. He never noticed me stand up or the crewman from the slaver that came upon him either with a pistol drawn. I saw Ignazio's eyes widen as the faces began to appear in the looking glass and I saw the pistol fire and those chunks of metal and glass as they tore a hole through his chest and his blood sprayed in a crimson arc upon the deck.

I threw my knife then and it stuck with a thud in the merchant sailor's forehead. It caused him to fall over in a heap as Ignazio staggered towards the rail with his eyes filling with those familiar questions and then he slumped over the rail and fell headlong into the depths of the angry sea. Without thinking I dove after him. Everything seemed surreal as I plunged towards the water and then the world was silent and my eyes were burning in their frantic hunt for the mirror. I swam deeper and deeper until I saw him slowly drifting downwards to the unknown fathoms below. His eyes were wide and his mouth was open and there in his hand was the mirror and so I pulled it from his grip and began to swim towards the surface.

In that moment something held me though, had me stop and look down as Ignazio slipped further away. I watched him slipping silently, the form slowly fading to a shadow in the deep and then he was gone. But I understood then that I had lost more than my friend. Something else had died and sank to the bottom of the sea and that was the last of who I was as a man. From that moment forward I gave myself over to the looking glass completely. It ruled everything, every decision, every action, every facet of my existence, everything but the guilt. The guilt belonged to me alone and so that guilt has led me here."

Chapter 8

Elias sat upright, stretching his back for a moment, then he placed the bottle to his lips and guzzled the Irish whiskey until it was empty, throwing the bottle on the floor and belching loudly as he did this and with a misty look in his eyes he grabbed the cigarettes, pulling one from the pack and lighting it. He took a long drag from the smoke, running his fingers through his hair several times before he stood up and grabbed the pack of cigarettes again. Then he grabbed the unopened bottle of Bushmills and walked across the room, stepping over Robert's legs and sitting down beside him.

He was silent as he smoked. The memories weighed heavily on his mind and the pain swelled in his eyes as he watched the smoke from his cigarette twist and coil into the air. He thought of ending it right then, of smashing the mirror and finishing the thing. Then he pulled the looking glass from the front of his pants and keeping it face down he looked at the carving of the young man who was trapped in that eternal stare and he tried to muster the strength to smash it, but he couldn't do it.

"You know, Robert," he said, clearing his throat and setting the mirror on the floor. "After I returned to Puerto Rico I took all of the wealth I had accumulated along with various tools such as an ax and a shovel and I left Lafitte's crew. I took it all into the jungle there and after searching for some time I found an elevated area and I built a rude home where I sat meditating on the mirror. For a long time I would not look into the pane of it, but when the dreams began again I looked and I gasped with the horror of my own reflection and I certainly wept for my own vanity, but then I looked deeper. It was in this meditation that I found I could do more than just sense those who had held the mirror before me. I could see them. In fact, sometimes I could actually see through them as though I were inside their minds and seeing what they were seeing.

After discovering this I set about moving and fortifying my home so that there was but one way in and one way out and this was through a gate of cliffs that ascended a good forty feet on either side with a lush jungle floor between and with a cutlass I cleared a path. Once this work was complete I set to focusing on the mirror again. I sat like this for several days until I saw the Roman, Licinius Cassius Sabaco come ashore. He had been sailing relentlessly about, just as I had, our paths likely crossing many of times without either of us being aware, but this time his ship had ported in Fajardo and it was obvious that he could sense the presence of the looking glass and thus he could sense the presence of me.

Licinius pushed and cut his way through the jungle and as he did this I went to the opening of the cliff walls and I waited. When he emerged and stepped into the clearing he found me sitting on a stone and smoking a cigar. He laughed when he saw me and shook his head.

"Hola, mi amigo."

"Hello, Elias," he said. "Did you honestly think you could hide from me in the jungle?"

"Yes, I did."

"There's not a place on earth that you could hide," he said, his skin like leather around the folds in his face. "If you just give me the mirror then maybe you won't lose anymore of your pretty parts." He laughed under his breath when said this and then he stepped closer.

"Well, you're going to have to catch me," I told him as I puffed on the cigar, "and I don't think you can do that."

When I said this he stopped laughing and scowled and then he began to run towards me. I flicked my cigar towards him and then I began to run. In my mind I had the image of the lion again, of his breathing as he chased me. I sprinted with the brush swiping my legs and the cut vegetation crushing beneath my boots until I reached a turn in the cliff walls and once around the bend I leapt forward and placed a foot on a small rock ledge and sprung again so that I landed back on the trail around ten feet from where I had left it. I could hear Licinius coming behind me, his heaviness treading as he came and then there was the sound that I had longed for, of the lion falling. There was the crash, the sound of the spears puncturing his flesh as he fell into the pit and then I was there standing above it. But in the pit, when I looked down, there was no lion, only a man.

How odd it was to see him there, gored as he was, for when Licinius fell he had gone in twisting and so the spears jutted out of his flesh in a manner that captured and froze him in a profoundly grotesque and unnatural pose. There were two spears in his head, which had landed on its right side, one exiting near his ear and the other through his jaw where it met the neck. From there his body began to rotate with spears entering his shoulder and exiting through his chest as his left arm dangled behind him unscathed. There were five shafts that had gone clean through his stomach and pelvis area with two others sticking out of his right leg and a large gouge in his left leg where the spear had caught the meat of his thigh and simply ripped it open.

To my great satisfaction he began to moan and wriggle like a worm strung on a hook and so I told him, "Don't go anywhere, Licinius. I shan't be long." When I returned I had a small keg of lamp oil, which I proceeded to pour over him as his body tensed and his loose arm flailed and then I sat down on the keg and withdrew another cigar and a box of matches. Then I placed the cigar in my mouth and took a stick match from the box and proceeded to tell him that I had gone to a great amount of trouble for his arrival, for it had taken some time to dig this pit and fashion those spears. Then I asked him, "Do you know Virgil," thumbing at the match as I spoke. "He wrote a handsome fabrication of your civilizations birth; the Aeneid is what it was called, I believe. There is an appropriate line, from that timeless piece, that suits this auspicious occasion and, if my memory serves me, it went 'I feel again the spark of an ancient flame'. Rather striking, don't you think?"

As I said this my thumbnail caught the match head with a pop and a hiss as the stick ignited. I brought it slowly to my cigar and puffed and from the pit I heard a low gurgled howl and then I dropped the match. It landed on his chest catching fire the oil soaked shirt and then the flames crawled along his body in either direction. Within minutes the entire pit was engulfed and wanting to ensure his destruction I placed the keg into the fire along with every type of loose brush or branch the jungle could afford me. I kept the fire burning for seven days. Vigilance was everything for me and when the fire died and the pit cooled I sifted through the ashes.

There was scarcely a bone to be found, but I dug the ashes up, placing them in leather satchels and then scattered them in the jungle. When my work was done I took the fragments of his skull and I cast them into the ocean and like many of the people in Puerto Rico, at the time, I did not change. I simply existed. I went on with each day mirroring the last with the sun shining down on me as I meditated on the looking glass, searching in its darkness with only one thought on my mind and that was to destroy all those who had come before me.

What I found was that several of the others had already met with some form of demise and that now only a handful of them remained. Horatio Seymour was one of these men. The more I focused on Seymour the more I realized that he was oblivious to me, to the others and to the looking glass itself. I became obsessed with him. The idea of this man began to fill every waking moment of my life

The Reflection of Elias Dumont

His skin was taut to his bones like a leathery paper-mache. He had the look of a mummy stripped of his wrappings and in the orbital sockets of his skull the yellowed eyes bulged as his thin velum like eyelids blinked lethargically. I tried for weeks to enter his mind, to see what he could see, but it was to no avail. There was a wall of darkness with him or perhaps his mind was a vacuous place, devoid of any thought or feeling. I did not know. It ate at me, my friend, like a tick under my skin - it ate at me.

When I could take it no longer I packed up my belongings and left for New York. The sea was green and calm that morning and it was good to be back onboard a ship. The *Orestes* was a merchant brig captained by Jose' Montez. It was a beautiful vessel with two square rigged masts and a large crew. I paid my way in gold and for the most part enjoyed a leisurely sail, as we stopped once in Virginia before heading further up the Eastern coast. Within a month's time we had reached New York Harbor at the mouth of the Hudson and as Montez called for the anchor to be dropped I watched the sun set, its oranges and yellows shimmering in the choppy dark waters and I listened to the waves break against the hull with a rhythmic lapping and I took in the smell of the harbor, the pungent odor of rotting sea mingled with sewage.

An evil was air about the place. It made me feel at home, with its seething criminal element and so I took up a vile and regrettable lifestyle here. 1841 New York was the perfect place for the looking glass to foster my greed, to cultivate every form of selfishness within me and I loved it. Within a very short period of time I had managed my way into certain circles, as I was a beautiful charmer, a man fully aware of his capabilities and prowess. And I had taken the name Charles Van Horn, as he had the misfortune of being very wealthy and looking a great deal like me.

The killing did not stop with him though for as my popularity and my wealth grew so did my paranoia. In my mind, everyone was trying to get the mirror. Many a young man befriended me, asking always a myriad of financial questions, prying ever towards the secret of my success, but I was a man of few words and those who pressed too far, those who persisted in knowing the secret eventually found themselves floating in the Hudson."

Pausing, Elias drew a cigarette from the pack and as he lit it he looked at Robert and then he took a long draw from it, removing it from his mouth as he did so and tucking it into the corner of the dead man's mouth. It sagged perilously from the bellboy's inanimate lips. "Careful," Elias said. "These things will give you cancer." Then he pulled another from the pack and lit it and smoked.

"I met a man there named Poe," he continued. "He was an odd fellow, a writer you know. I think he liked me because I didn't talk much. I wasn't one to fawn all over him like the sycophantic dullards of those circles. I was someone he didn't have to say anything to. And he wasn't one to suckle my teat either.

No, Edgar was not one to ask anything about me nor was he one to ask anything of me, but I could see a curiosity at times, a subtle look about his eyes that questioned my devotion to him. He never found an answer and in the few and far days we spent together he introduced me to two things that had a cataclysmic effect upon my stay in New York.

The first of these things were the opium dens of Chinatown and the other was a woman named Mary Rogers. I spent a good amount of time in both of them as they were both always willing to receive me. Edgar and I would lie around for hours in the dens with the sweet opiate filling our lungs and the secret voice in my head filling me with delusions of grandeur, as if I were some magnanimous slayer. I would think about being the kindhearted killer as I lay there and I would laugh, stirring the involuntary laughter of Edgar and we would laugh until I fell into tears.

What came of this was my love for opium and for Mary, both of which came instantaneously upon the first tasting. Mary, however, had me with a smile. Her grin was dark and aloof and I could see why so many men wanted to buy their cigars from her. Edgar could see it too, the adulterous air that hovered around her, but Edgar did not see the note Mary placed in my cigar box.

I still don't understand the chemistry, why she decided to meet me that night after work when so many other prominent men had been chasing her. Perhaps it was something in the darkness of my eyes, something that was akin to her lips. But, we met that night and several other nights after as well, slipping through the shadows to avoid being seen by her family, her friends, the trove of acquaintances or neighbors who gossiped about her and the irksome man she was betrothed to marry.

Each night we met, Mary took me to a place by the river, a hollow in the tall weeds and bushes, a place she liked to go to when the cities women were scathing and the men were intolerable and the crime and the murder and the poverty seemed out of control and overwhelming, she liked it here by the river. I let her talk as we sat beneath the moonlight and then our passion would stir and I would have my way with her. Her skin was like milk beneath the moon or better she was a drop, a tear that had fallen from the moon and I was the devil that drank it.

We met five times in this manner and on the day of the fifth encounter I left a signature rose in her doors key hole to let her know I would be there, in our place by the river. The weather that night was bad and for I time I sat on the stones in that hollow and thought she would not come and as my mind drifted across the darkness of the Hudson, where the intermittent slivers of silver broke as the pale moon slid arduously through the nimbus clouds, I began thinking about Horatio Seymour and why I had not been able to discover him.

The thought of him perplexed me. I began to think that perhaps he had left New York, that perhaps he had sensed my presence there and moved on in his vagabond way. Confident I would hear Mary coming, I

The Reflection of Elias Dumont

slid the looking glass from the front of my pants, turning it over so that my reflection appeared. A mist gathered on the pane as I stared at the truth of my existence, the horrible reality of my condition. On the left side of my neck a large tumor, the size of an orange, had bloomed. Another cyst the size of an egg rose above my left ear, which further magnified my deplorable appearance. I now looked like something from other than this world, something inhuman or alien to nature and so I became anxious and the need for the opium swelled and the tears rolled with anger down my face, acidic and bitter and then I felt her hand on my shoulder.

There was a gasp and a faint cry as Mary bent and saw my image in the looking glass. I felt the mirror slip from my fingers as the night went silent and every second moved like an eternity; my body turning as she stumbled backwards and my hands moving in concert with the swaying whisper mirror, its words manipulating every movement as if the voice from the looking glass were some djinn whose powers pulled the wires of the cosmos.

As I strangled her, Mary became the haunting apparition of Aurore. Her face was shadowed and the hair fell all around it as my fingers squeezed her warm skin and I cursed and growled, "Why won't you die?" But, she had died, just as every woman I open myself to dies, as if they were all linked somehow, a single spirit caught in a perpetual loop of terror, cursed to enter each new vessel only so that I may rip them from it again. I wept as I kissed her, the tears staining my cheeks and her cheeks and I could taste those saline kisses as I inhaled the perfume of her body and those lifeless eyes filled with darkness and the specter like fragments of the moon, my tremulous hands ravaging her dress, tearing it in strips like a mad animal would and then the deed was over.

I could not look at her as I slid her corpse into the river. I could not watch her drift away into the darkness, into the ethereal realm like a spirit set to cross the Styx. I could not look at her. So I stood at the edge amongst the weeds and the crickets and in the bleak light that fluctuated on the black and blue skin of the river I found my reflection, a lucent shade, its calamitous features distorted in the rippling water and there it stood looking at me and it was laughing.

There is much after that in which I do not recall. I could not tell you when I left the bank of the Hudson or when I retrieved the mirror. I do not remember leaving that place, Mary's hollow, or how I got to the opium den. Three days were lost in the fog of that opiate. I smoked it without any concern for life or love and as I drew from the pipe I felt my heart stop and my lungs asphyxiate while there, in the doorway to my chamber, stood Horatio Seymour.

Had I not already soiled my pants I would have then. He stood silent in the door and as he did this I choked for air, but my body was dying its natural death, if one could call drinking, smoking and drugging yourself to death natural, but Horatio stood there, the overseer of my mortal ending.

"Take it," I gasped, attempting to sit forward. "Take it. It's yours."

He said nothing.

"You know what I speak of. Take it. I am ruined for it."

But the man said nothing and then he was gone.

It took me another day to gain enough strength to leave. Worse yet was the absence of my heartbeat. It was an unnerving thing, to be so conscious of my death, to know that I was no longer alive and that it was only the mirror that sustained me. Most are not aware of their hearts, the constant rhythm inside of them; that pulse in their veins as it sings through their body. Most don't hear it in the waken state unless they exert themselves, cause it to beat harder than normal and they do not hear it when they lay down to go to sleep, like I often did. Believe me though. When it is gone you are fully aware."

As Elias said this he pressed the bottle of Bushmills to his lips and poured. Bubbles of air drifted through the liquid as he guzzled and when the bottle was empty he tipped it again, licking the rim with his tongue and then he peered inside the empty bottle, as if in disbelief. Then, smiling, he looked at the label of the bottle and said, "It's not that the alcohol circulates so much as it saturates my body." Then he laughed and flopped the empty bottle onto the bed and shifting his weight to his left side he turned and looked at Robert.

The cigarette in the dead bellboy's mouth had burned down to the butt and there dangling from his lips was a long and pristine ash.

"You look like you've been on one hell of a bender, my friend," Elias said laughing. Then he stood up, stretched and placed another cigarette in his own mouth as he sat on the edge of the bed. "You know I did end up finding Mr. Seymour," he continued. "I found him one evening as I wondered aimlessly around the city, aimless in that I did not concern myself with where the Katoptron took me, as it nearly always seemed to carry me along in its strange and unpredictable agenda. But that evening I happened upon a museum of oddities. It stood opposite St. Paul's Chapel at Broadway and Vesey Street like some great instrument of chaos. It was the yin to the churches yang. I had read of Barnum's museum, but it really had not interested me until I stood outside the door. There was a strange feeling as I stood there. It was like something cold had entered my bones.

Without really thinking I filed in with the steady stream of people, the men with their goatees, top hats and coats and the woman all dressed in their gilded coats of fur, each of us shifting in the bedlam of the traffic, of the elaborate carriages, of horses with plumes of feathers in their manes, in the cacophony of the bustling intersection, all of us paying our quarters to behold the spectacle that it was, the myriad of oddities, the remains of the so called Fiji mermaid, the one-hundred sixty-one year old nurse of George Washington. Joice Heth was her name, a sham Barnum billed as "Unquestionably the most astonishing and

The Reflection of Elias Dumont

interesting curiosity in the world!" But it was in the dim shadows of a room that I found him.

He was silent as he stood with the crowd of gentlemen around him and the women, with their hands over their faces and their fingers slightly parted, he stood there. Horatio Seymour, one of, "500,000 natural and artificial curiosities from every corner of the globe," and then the audience shuddered as he pierced his skin with a long needle, pressing it through one side of the arm and out the other. He then did this to his face, pressing the silver into his right cheek until the audience could see the point upon his tongue and then he pushed it on and out of the left cheek. The men whispered to one another how there was no blood. Not a drop of blood spilled from a single piercing of that strange hide. It had them in all manners of awe and confusion, but I understood it.

Horatio Seymour was dead. He was as dead as I was, more so in fact. It brought a smile to my face as I thought about it. "Bravo," I applauded as he withdrew each of the long needles and placed them meticulously parallel to one another on the table beside him. It caused the rest of the gathering to applaud and move towards the exit signs. The women, with their grotesque faces, bantering about the incomprehensibilities of the show, how ghastly it was and yet the men found the sepulchral gimmick jocular.

Had they but known the truth of it. Had they but understood that they were in the midst of not just one monster, not one freak of nature, but two. Two unholy things, one suffering as the other mused. So close to death they were. One never really knows who they are standing next to in a crowd.

I waited until they all had left the room and then I clapped again and smiled.

"What do you want?" he said.

"I just want to talk to you."

"Is it here?"

"You know that it is."

"Get it away from me. I will not talk to you so long as you have it."

"Why were you watching me?"

Horatio stood silent.

"I saw you. Outside of my room, in the den, I saw you."

Still he said nothing. His eyes glared at me like to ocher spheres in the dim light. In the hall I could hear another group coming, their footsteps heavy on the wood floor.

"Tell me, Horatio. Why were you there, on Mott St. at the opium joint? Why didn't you take it?"

But, the crowd entered and his face remained frozen, like something petrified over time. I looked at him again, huffing as I did so and then I nodded and turned and walked towards the exit. It was as I was leaving that I heard it. The mirror tried to confuse it, tried to speak over it, but I heard it. It was Horatio Seymour's voice. It crept into my mind like the wind through and old window. He told me to leave the mirror and then he beckoned me to come when the museum was closed.

When I returned, it was sometime after midnight. On my hands was the smell of sex and opium and of death. This was the smell of New York, a smell that saturated my clothes, my skin and my wretched psyche. I inhaled this scent with the cold air as I wrapped on the back door to the museum. For a moment I thought he would not come, but then I heard the latch and the door creek open; saw his owl eyes in the darkness glaring at me. So I stepped in and closed the door.

He held an oil lamp in his hand and without saying a word he turned and began to walk slow and fragile through the dim hall. On our right in a parlor sat a woman who appeared to be over five-hundred pounds and as the appearance of her gave me a start I noticed she was speaking to two men who appeared to be joined at the shoulder or chest. They nodded at us as we passed them and then Horatio told them good night and opened a door to a room to let us in.

The room was not much bigger than a walk-in closet, but in it was a small cot covered with old newspapers. Beside the cot was a small round pedestal table made of cherry wood, which he sat the oil lamp on and then he handed me a fold out stool that I proceeded to open and place beside the table. He bid me to sit with a gesture of his hand and so I did and then he asked me if I wanted some tea, explaining that it was just steeped and that it would do me good.

I accepted the offer, allowing Horatio to pour us both a cup before he sat down on the cot with the papers rustling beneath him and then he sipped the tea as I pulled a flask from my coat and tipped a bit of whiskey into the warm fluid. He gave a solitary chuckle when I did this and then I offered him a nip as well, but he waved it off.

"I am glad you did not bring it here," he said.

"Yes," I answered, sipping my tea. "That's an interesting scar you have on your neck."

"Yes," he answered. "A priest, Videl Moratelli did this to me."

"Videl?"

"Yes," he said, the thin eyebrows rising above his bulging eyes. "You know of him?"

"I am familiar with him, but how did he give you that scar?"

The Reflection of Elias Dumont

"My family brought him to me, upon the advice of my evening nurse, a woman who claimed to be from the local convent. She had offered to help my mother so that she could get some rest."

"But, why?"

"They performed an exorcism on me, to dispel the demon that had possessed me. They did this because, I heard a voice in my head; a voice that told me to do terrible things, sir; things I could not bring myself to do."

"But, the scar?"

"I do not remember it all, for they had me bound and they had given me a tincture of opium to relax me."

"Yes."

"And as the nurse veiled my eyes I told her that it was the mirror that I had found, the beautiful mirror and that it had placed the voice in my head, but she soothed me with her voice and the gentleness of her touch and on her was a sweet smell, like that of a bouquet of flowers and I could hear the priest as he spoke in Latin. Then his knife opened my neck and the blood rushed out as he bellowed to the lord that they must bleed the demon out. And so, I was bled, bled of every last drop of my blood."

"And Videl took the looking glass?

"Yes."

"But, how did you know me?"

"I have known many like you Elias Dumont, many who have come looking for me, just as you did, but none of them had what you have."

"And what is that," I said, tipping the tea cup back and emptying it into my throat.

"A conscience, Elias. None of them had remorse for their actions…"

"How do you know this of me!"

"… None of them felt the burden of guilt as you do."

"Damn you. You old fool," I growled, standing up from the stool as I said it. "You don't know about me. You know absolutely nothing about me. I am a devil, a killer, a madman and I certainly feel no remorse for it."

"Really," he said. "I know you killed Mary Rogers, Elias."

When he said this a chill went through my body and then I sat back down, taking the flask out again and unscrewing the cap and drinking as he spoke.

The Reflection of Elias Dumont

"I saw you there that night, at the edge of the Hudson river," he continued. "I watched you strangle that woman, but I saw something else as well. I saw your tears. I saw the hurt in you as you placed her in the river, as your mind collapsed, as you wondered about the night until you ended up there in Chinatown lying on that bed with the Asian screens above you and the opium boiling over the oil lamp, the opium that you inhaled so that you might blot out the pain and the anger and the guilt. There I saw a bit of myself in you."

"It controls nearly all of my actions," I told him.

"Yes, Elias. You must destroy it. You must smash this mirror and end this nightmare for all of us or it will continue and the world will suffer it as we suffer it."

"You would have me commit suicide."

He laughed as I said this and then he sat his tea cup on the pedestal table. "I think we both understand that you are already dead, Elias."

The thought of it was gut wrenching, I began ringing my cursed hands as my nerves unraveled. I hated thinking of it, the absence of my heart beat; the deafening silence of it. "I must leave you now," I told him, standing up again and rushing to the door.

"Wait, Elias," he said.

But, it was too late. I ran out the door as the bewildered eyes of the freaks needled over my skin and the anxiety bore down so that the hall grew smaller until I reached the door and turned the knob and fell into the cold damp street. But, it was over and I needed the looking glass, its reassurance, the comfort it gave me like the comfort of the bourbon. Then I wept until I fell asleep and in my dreams I heard Horatio's voice and I knew that he was right.

The following day he was gone. I paid a quarter to go through, to see him again, but his corner was empty save the table and the needles. It put me in a bitter mood and as two women raved about the Fiji mermaid I growled at them, "It's just a damn fish with a monkey head attached to it, you imbeciles." The women blubbered when I said this and then I pushed my way out and into the street again.

I would not see Horatio Seymour again until 1944. Curiously, he had joined the Ringling Brothers and Barnum & Bailey circus, performing with the freaks again in the side show. It was mere happenstance that I saw his picture on a post in the town of Hartford, Connecticut, a town I would have only passed through, but there he was. So I went to the grounds off Barbour St. and began to ask around for the Ring Master. It struck me as something I might enjoy, traveling with the circus and I could confide in Horatio and perhaps together I could raise the strength to end this, to find some type of redemption.

The Reflection of Elias Dumont

I was fortunate enough to come across Emmett Kelly, a sour looking hobo clown that pointed me in the direction of the Ring Master's trailer. I thanked him as he tipped his hat and then I made my way to the trailer, knocking on the door several times. When no one answered I opened the door, holding the screen with my foot as I said hello, but he was gone. Not thinking much of it I stepped inside, onto the warn out stained carpet and then I walked around looking at the memorabilia about his smoke yellowed walls. Yes, the circus I thought. So I sat down on his couch and waited.

It was no more than twenty minutes before he arrived. Huffing, the old man opened the screen door to his trailer, its hinges squeaking as it swung and then it clambered as the spring caught and the screen came back, hitting his elbow as he turned the handle to the door and stepped in. As he entered he pulled the red tie from around his neck and turned and slung it over a hook on the wall and then he smirked and straightened the picture hanging beside it.

The black and white picture was faded and yellowed, but he could still see the Human Conundrum standing there beside him, his entire body covered in nails and pins. He got lost in the picture for a moment, twirling his long black coiled mustache as nostalgia swept him into better times and the sounds of the center ring. He was just grasping the bill of his top hat when he heard the sound of my boot buckle jingle slightly. The old man turned with a proper ease and straitened, holding the lapels of his jacket with his hands.

"May I help you sir?"

"Yes," I said. "I'm looking for work."

"Well, I can't help you with that so you'll need to be on your way."

"I was told that you were the man to see."

"Yes," he said; the light dulling from his eyes as he cleared his throat. "This morning I was the man to see, but now I am not." Grinning again he pulled on the cuffs of his jacket and turned once more towards the picture. "What's your talent if you don't mind me asking?" he continued, removing his hat as he said it.

My knife caught the black top hat and stuck it to the wall before he could reach the hook to hang it. He looked at it for a moment and then at me, his thick gray eyebrows raised and then he turned and went into the kitchen and lifted an old pot of coffee from the burner of the stove and looked inside. He then asked me if I cared for a cup, placing it back on the burner and I told him thank you but no. After a few minutes it began to boil and he poured a cup out and sat it on the small metal dining room table.

"So, who do I see then if you're not the man to see?"

"You'll have to talk to the owners," He said, pulling a bottle of whisky from the counter and pouring a bit into his coffee. "You'll find them in the tent just up

The Reflection of Elias Dumont

from the lion cages," he continued, picking the coffee cup up from the table and taking a sip. "I just came from there so if you hurry along you may catch them."

I got up then and walked across the room and pulled the knife out of his hat and hung the hat on the hook. "Just up from the lions then?"

"Yes," he said, regaining a bit of his composer for posterity.

With a nod I opened the door and stepped out, closing the door behind me. I felt sorry for him, for his aging and for the way he seemed to be giving into it and then I made my way towards the music and the big top. What fate or god or devil determined that I should remain exquisite for eternity while everyone else around me withered and died. It was both gratifying and perplexing.

When I reached the lion's cage I felt a chill. There were two of them lying as if sedated, their great mains a matted shock around their yawning jowls, but a third one stood motionless. It was a heavy beast and as it stood I could see the definition of its muscles, the tension in them as he peered at the big top and then I got the chill again. It caused me to turn and look at the big top as well.

It was a massive thing with American flags waving above it and hundreds of people filing in, all of them there to see the greatest show on earth. I felt a sudden need to see it, to go there beneath the great tent and all the while the mirror whispered, yes.

By the time I got in the show had begun. It was a spectacle to behold as the high wire act, The Flying Wallendas, was just beginning and then I spotted Horatio. He was standing along the inner ring and there was a look of terror on his face as he looked about and then he stopped and his gaze fell to the far entrance. When he did this I looked as well and there standing in the opening was Videl.

He wore a black stovepipe hat with a rim that casted a shadow over his face and as he stood there the wind rippled his long black trench coat so that it slapped about at the center of his boots. Though I could not see his face, I knew he was staring at Horatio and then I moved in closer. When I did this Videl's head rose so that I could just see the flare in his eyes and then he lifted his hand and popped open the lid to a Zippo lighter. There was a brief pause and then he struck the flint wheel which sent a plume of flames racing up the canvas tent wall.

Within a matter of minutes the entire big top was engulfed in flames. The fire raced and exploded with and inconceivable voracity as the canvas had, regrettably, been waterproofed with gasoline and paraffin wax. I wanted to run to Horatio, to pull him out of the inferno, but he just stood there looking up with his arms raised. He stood there as over a hundred men women and children were crushed and burned to death. So, I ran with the stampede. I ran while the center pole erupted in flames and the tent came crashing down. I ran. And, that was my first encounter with Videl.

Chapter 9

It was 8:11 in the evening when Elias left the hotel again. There was a light rain coming down as he walked, it made the denim of his jacket feel heavy, but he liked the feeling of it. He liked it because it meant he could still feel; that he had not lost that part of himself yet and so he walked with his hands tucked in the pockets of the jacket. A scattering of colors followed him in the wet blacktop as he walked, an ever shifting reflection, but he paid no mind to it. He just wanted to catch a cab.

He made it as far as Laclede's Landing before he stopped on the old cobblestones of Lucas St. and looked down the hill at the flood waters. The dark muddy liquid glistened as it seized control of the buildings and the wharf. It sent a chill over him. Elias wanted a drink, but there was no time for it. Echo would be waiting for him and so he turned, walking up Lucas, then across North 2nd St. until he reached Morgan where he recognized the old Schoelhorn-Albrecht building, a place he had worked at for a short time making capstans for the barges; a place that had secret rooms for concealing run-away slaves.

Pausing again, he looked up at the building as the rain beaded on his face and then he looked around at the sidewalk, tilting his head as he observed the unevenness of it. He thought of the slaves and their terrible condition, packed in a room below the cobblestones, just as they were packed into the ships that delivered them to this nightmare. He thought of the mirror then too and how he was a slave to it and then he pressed his hands further into the pockets of his coat and walked again. He walked until a cab came up to the curb at 3rd St. and without hesitation Elias opened the door and slid in.

"Alabama Ave," Elias said, pushing his wet hair back. "The bridge over the River des Peres."

The cabby barely nodded as he depressed the meter and then his eyes shifted with a glance in the rearview mirror. He was a large man with a full beard and he was wearing a bright yellow Ted Drewes Frozen Custard shirt, which was a size too small for him, but he was quiet and Elias was glad for that. The only sound came from the road and the occasional swipe of the windshield wiper blades.

By 9:30 they were on the bridge and Elias could see Echo's slender form standing patiently at the end. She was positioned with her back against the rain and he could just see her eyes beneath the rim of the green, 1940's style, Cloche hat she wore. She was gorgeous, he thought and then the cab stopped and Elias swung the door open.

"Do you need a lift miss?" he said smirking.

"No thank you. I prefer walking," she answered, placing the cigarette that rested in her fingers between the moist lips of her mouth.

"Shall I join you then?"

"You shall," she said, blowing the smoke out as she smiled.

Getting out of the cab, Elias pulled his money clip from his front pocket and snapping the bills loose he handed them through the open window of the cab. The cabby leaned and took the bills with a nod and then the window went back up as the cab pulled away. Elias turned then and placed his foot on the concrete base of the guard rail and gazed southward down the River des Peres.

Power-lines stretched along either side of the hemorrhaging river. He let his eyes follow the edge where the water pushed against miles of sandbags, all stacked atop the insufficient levees. Then Echo leaned against him and pitched her cigarette over the side and putting her hand in his she began to walk back across the bridge.

"You know, I did kill her," Elias said as he walked beside Echo and the rain came down, shimmering like silver beads beneath the overhanging street lights.

"I know," she said.

"But, I didn't just kill Ha'-ba-tu. You see, when I had my back to her, when I was so absorbed with myself, she picked up the knife that I had left on the ground and like a graceful silent deer she leapt and plunged the knife into my back. I felt the burn and the tare of it as it went in and then I spun around and she was standing there motionless.

What I did next was unspeakable. I went at her with all the new appetites of my immortality, stripping her as she clawed at me, her softness folding around me as my hands held her by the neck and I took her. Our bodies meshed under the shock of the moon and the cold air caught our breath and hung it like a mournful veil around us until I could last no more, dying as only a lover could die and then her breath ran out and the

The Reflection of Elias Dumont

heavens seemed littered with silver daggers. I remember how utterly unreal it felt as I reached over my shoulder, grasping the handle of the blade, pulling it lose from my body and then collapsing beside her.

In the morning I awoke against her pale cold breast. I believe I was in a fit of shock when I saw her, the bruises on her neck and the realization of what I had done and what I had become sank in. I gathered my things hastily and packed them on the horse again. Then, I went about gathering soft green twigs until I had enough to make a wreath, which I fitted to Ha'-ba-tu's head. She looked beautiful as I gathered her into my arms and carried her to the edge of the river. For a moment I knelt and then I asked god to forgive me as the body floated out and down with the current, drifting away until the sight of her was gone. But, what I found, Echo, was that the sight of her never left my mind. She is still there, forever adrift in that river.

When I reached my home in New Madrid I'd been gone for three days. My body ached as I tied the horse Ka'-wa-ska had given me to the post. The horse shied away from me again, its two front hooves stammering and its large brown bulbous eye averting. Then, I secured the rope and made a clicking sound with my mouth to settle the horse. She did not like me touching her as I had well learned. I held a hand on her main for a moment then attempted to bring the trunk down from her back as a group of men approached me from the front porch. One of them was my bother Joseph.

"Elias, is that you?' Joseph said as he threw his cigar to the ground.

Looking over my shoulder, I turned and let my hand slide down the side of the horse. "Yes it's me, Joseph," I replied, turning back to my work of getting the trunk down.

"Mother's going to be so happy to see you," he said. "We all thought, well, we..."

"You thought what?"

"Well, we thought you were dead," he muttered, his eyes glassy as he moved closer to me.

"Well, I didn't," I scoffed. "Somebody want to give me a hand with this?"

"Sure son," my uncle replied, grabbing one of the leather straps that held the trunk. "You're going to want to go inside though. There is something you need to know."

"What I need is this trunk down Francois," I remarked, narrowing my eyes at him. "I will go in when the trunk is down and I can take it with me."

"As you wish," he sighed. "Go to the other side and I will undo the straps."

When he said this I pushed between Francois and the horse and as I reached the rear there was a faint twitch in its tail and then the shoe struck me like a bolt of lightning. The kick threw me a good fifteen feet. All I saw was light as I lay in a heap on the cold ground. I thought about how stupid that was. I may as well have kicked myself and then I began to laugh. There was a ringing in my ears and then I saw my brother standing over me, mouthing some inaudible panic. Dazed, I didn't want to move, but the men picked me up and carried me into the house, slamming open the front door

The Reflection of Elias Dumont

as we came. I saw my uncle Francois waving someone out of the chair in the front room and then they sat me down.

"Are you alright, Elias?" Joseph asked with his hand on my shoulder.

Like a madman I just tipped my head forward and sat up in the chair, my hair falling over my eyes as my hands pressed against the seat and the laughter escaped my odd grin. "Did you get my trunk?" but everyone in the room stood in silent awe.

"I ain't never seen nobody get kicked like that and live to tell it," Francois said finally, scratching his forehead as he looked at me. "I sure as hell never seen anyone laugh about it either."

Another of the men was questioning the absence of a mark on my head when my mother came into the room. She was wailing and pushing them out of the way as she came towards me. Then she held me and kissed me and her eyes moved like a flock of sparrows and I understood then that my father was dead.

I stood up as she held my hand and then I walked soberly through the room and into the parlor where they had him laid out. I had come home to a wake and there, sitting next to him was Aurore.

She fell into tears when she saw me and I held her to me as I looked over my father. He was barely forty-five, I thought. Death I pondered, death was something I would never know. This thing or place or even perhaps this experience called death was nothing to me now for I was born into a new and everlasting existence. So I picked my father's pipe up from the table where it sat and I looked at him again as he lay cold and stiff with his gray skin and yellowed fingernails and I tried to cry, I tried, but I could not. So, I turned, pulling myself away from Aurore and then I walked away.

"Where are you going?" she said, her eyes swollen with tears.

"To my room," I said. "I need to be alone."

It was over then. I should have known it. I should have grabbed the trunk and rode away that very moment, but I didn't, I stayed. It was my own greed that kept me there. My selfish desire for her outweighed all of my logic. I knew the mirror wanted her dead. There wasn't a day after that fatal arrival home that it didn't urge me to kill her. But, I loved her, I wanted her and I was going to have her no matter the costs."

As they came to the corner of Davis St. and Alabama, Elias stepped off the sidewalk, pulling Echo along with him, their heals clapping on the wet road as they crossed the street. In the middle of Alabama was a round concrete barrier that was painted yellow, assumingly to warn off traffic, but the stop sign in the center of it was bent like an old woman's spine. Echo looked at it as they passed and then Elias opened the door to the *Last Stop Liquor and Live Bait* store. It felt good for him to get out of the rain and he needed a drink desperately. The rain seemed nothing to her though, her lamia skin, impregnable to the elements and Elias felt it as his fingers slid from hers and he looked at her face as it glistened like virgin olive oil and the cheeks flushed with a newborn's rouge.

Elias could tell she had fed well, there was certainly another corpse in the river, he thought as he asked the man behind the counter for a bottle of Wild Turkey and a pack of Lucky Strikes. He wondered how she viewed things, how she viewed him. What was the attraction for her? Certainly another lamia would be more suitable.

"I hope the rain lets up," the man said from behind the counter as he laid the cigarettes down.

"Yes," Echo answered. "River des Peres looks like it's going to burst."

"I sure hope it don't ma'am," he added, sliding the bottle of bourbon into a sack and placing it on the counter. "Everybody's been working hard to keep them sandbags up."

"Well," Elias said as he handed the man some money. "When a river has it in its mind to do something nothing can stop it."

The man opened the register and placed the bills in the slots and then he counted the change out and looked at the two strangers. His unibrow rose as he looked at them, with its curious scar above the left eye. It caused the right brow to appear to be usurping the left as if it had grown across and gradually pushed the other into its dwarfed state. He then proceeded to count the change back into Elias's hand. He was a bit miffed by the comment and didn't quite know how to respond.

"You all have a good evening," he said, closing the register as he said it.

"Thank you," Elias said, picking up the cigarettes and the bourbon as he stepped away from the counter and left the store.

Outside a light mist still saturated the darkness. Elias tucked the bottle under his armpit and opened the pack of cigarettes, then he took one out and lit it. As he placed the pack into the inside pocket of his coat Echo began to cross Davis St. He watched her walk for a moment, folding the sack down and unscrewing the cap to the bourbon as his eyes followed her curves and then placed the bottle to his lips and drank.

"Quit staring at my ass," she said, "…and come on."

Smiling, Elias took another drink. Then he placed the cigarette back into his mouth and went after her. They walked a good distance as Elias told her about Aurore and how the two of them had continued to plan their wedding despite his father's funeral. The two of them lived with Elias's mother and brother, which became immediately difficult for him as he grew more obsessed with himself and more suspecting of others.

Elias explained how his mothers constant questioning of him led him to believe that she knew. The looking glass compounded this effect, always whispering in his mind that she knew he had changed, that she knew about the mirror and that she would take it from him and cast it away. As Elias's paranoia grew his mother's questions came more often, each of them probing further, each of them driving him to madness until he knew what he had to do.

The Reflection of Elias Dumont

He told Echo of the nightshade he had found, the *belladonna* he said and how he had, under the instruction of the mirror, gathered the berries and ground them, pouring the juice into his mother's wine. The next day the doctor pronounced her dead from fever. He recalled the looking glass praising him as they placed her in the ground, with all the mourners weeping around him and him watching the dirt land on her casket as he smiled.

Worse yet was his brother Joseph, for he had glimpsed the sinister look upon Elias's face and thus had truly fueled a justified suspicion. It prompted Joseph to move out of the house, with him telling Elias at the door as he left that he didn't know who he was anymore, that he was sinister and that he would prove him to be so. Elias said nothing as he watched his brother walk away. He looked unreal, like a mannequin in the doorway, as Joseph glanced back and then turned and left the home of his father.

Elias drank heavily as he told Echo this, smoking one cigarette after another until they reached Schirmer St. where they took a right and then she led him to Michigan Ave. and into St Boniface Catholic church, with its two towers rising on either side and the crosses high atop their posts. He felt a shudder as he walked into the foyer, but he wasn't sure if it was from the dampness of his clothes or his own evil presence in god's home.

"I like to come here sometimes," Echo whispered as they sat on the left pew in the back row. "I like to watch the people here with all of their rituals. It helps me..." she said pausing.

Elias looked apathetically across the pews to the small alter adorned with white linen and silver. Everything appeared old to him or aging, everything seemed to be dying, the two old women kneeling towards the front, the priest praying over the rows of tall blue candle holders where the flock pays to have their prayers come true, everything was old but Echo. Even he was aging and he understood this. His beauty was but window dressing. But Echo, she had truly stopped aging. Her beauty transcended time, with all of its lush vitalities and the rhythmic pulse of her heart that he could feel in the palm of his hand as she held it in hers. He wanted that.

He leaned then closer to her and kissed her lightly on the cheek and then he rose, genuflecting as he left the pew and then he walked up the aisle and over to the candles. The priest had just finished meditating as Elias pulled his money clip from his pocket and pulled the rest of the money from it, stuffing it into the donation box, "To the everlasting life," he said and then he set to lighting the rest of the unlit candles.

The priest said something to him, but he wasn't listening. He was absorbed in the flames, in the glowing blue of the glass, of the smell of the match and the rich floral scent of incense that seemed to be infused into everything in the church. When he finished he realized that Echo was standing just behind and to the side of him and she was lost in the flames as well.

He placed his hand back in hers and when he did this she looked at him and he could see the candles refracting in her eyes like a burning kaleidoscope of black and blue, yellow, green and brown.

The Reflection of Elias Dumont

"You know I've brought harm to every woman I have ever loved," he said softly, their eyes locked together so that in the flames and the fragments he could see himself reflecting in her eyes, reflecting as their faces moved closer together.

"Yes," she sighed with her bosom swelling .and sinking like an ocean under the spell of the moon, the air moving into her and out while her lips parted like some sensuous red sea to deliver him from the pain and solitude of his servile existence.

When his lips pressed to hers the world fell into nonexistence and all the universe seemed to form around them. He felt like a chord in a song designed to instruct the cosmos, that every particle followed the movement of their tempo, slow and thaumaturgical. He felt alive. There was an energy about them, but he wondered in that instant if the energy was only hers, if this was just a spell that he was under. Was this what her victims felt? Was this the euphoria before the darkness?

Slowly, he pulled his lips from her lips and she placed her cheek against his cheek, her breath still heavy as she whispered, "I want to take you somewhere."

The two old women were glaring at them as they walked back down the center aisle. One of the ladies was giving Echo the evil eye as they passed. The other was speaking under her breath about the couple's behavior. Neither of them cared. Elias was enthralled with Echo and her with him as they opened the door to the church and stepped outside. He had left his bourbon in the pew, oblivious to it as they walked across the concrete and out onto Michigan Ave.

As they walked he told Echo about his brother Joseph and how he had accused Elias of having killed their mother. The mirror, all the while, demanding that Elias kill him, cursing him each time Elias let Joseph go. He explained that one evening Joseph had come to the house drunk and belligerent. He had a pistol in one hand and a skull in the other. To his horror it was the skull of William Ferro.

"I saw you bury this, brother," he yelled, holding the skull over his head. "It seems mother isn't the only person you've killed."

"You're drunk," Elias told him as he stepped onto the front porch, Aurore stepping out behind him as he drew his pistol.

"Does it bother you that your fiancée is a murderer?" Joseph said staggering.

"Stop this, both of you," Aurore screamed as she stepped off the porch.

"Can't you see that he's changed, that he's possessed, that he's the devil?"

"Mind your tongue before it gets you killed, brother."

"You would like that."

"What I would like is for you to go back to Uncle Francois's house and sleep it off."

"Yes. Please go home, Joseph," Aurore pleaded with her lips beginning to tremble.

The Reflection of Elias Dumont

"This skull was buried in the backyard," he said hurling the dismal thing at them. It tumbled grossly about on the ground until it came to rest near Aurore's feet.

"Is this true, Elias?" she said, turning towards him with shock and tears full in her eyes and as she did this Elias aimed and shot his brother in the head.

The shot caused Joseph's legs to fold so that his feet lay one beneath his thigh and the other sprawled out to the side. His arms were stretched out in either direction with the pistol still loosely clutched in his hand.

"You murdered him," she said trembling. "You murdered your own brother."

"He was going to kill me," he said as he stepped off the porch. "You saw him. There was no reasoning with him."

"He was drunk, Elias."

"Yes. But, this is how men settle things," he told her, squatting near his brothers head with the dark blood soaking into the earth beneath his boots.

"No," she said, her face distraught.

"I'll need to bring someone out so that we can give him a proper burial and clear ourselves of any wrong doing," he continued, but she wasn't listening. Instead she marched back into the house and in his mind the looking glass became frantic.

When Elias got into the house he could hear her tearing their bedroom apart. She was pulling the drawers from the chest and emptying them on the bed when he walked in. "You're looking for the mirror, aren't you?"

"The mirror?" she said.

"You can't have it," he growled, the words reverberating from those in his mind.

"You need help, Elias," Aurore wept.

At the corner of Michigan and Davis Echo stopped him. "Let it go, Elias," she said. "Let her go."

"But I strangled her, Echo," he said with pain seething wild in his eyes. "I loved her and I killed her and I have carried that guilt for almost two-hundred years." He let her hand go and walked away from her, his hands cupping over his eyes.

"You are a killer, Elias," Echo said, her voice firm and resolute.

"But, I wasn't supposed to be," he said turning towards her again. "I see her face in my mind. She haunts me, Echo. Those eyes; her terrible questioning eyes, I destroyed her and I cannot live with it again. I cannot do it again."

"And you won't," she said, moving to him as if she had slipped through a fold in space and time.

"I am not like you," he said. "Without the mirror I am nothing."

She took his hand again, but this time she urged him to run with her, through the back streets and the yards, with the puddles splashing beneath their feet and the dark and misty wind blowing in their face and ears until they reached an old abandoned building strangled with weeds and vines. She took him around to a loading area where the concrete was crumbling and as they climbed the stairs he could just see the swollen Mississippi in the distance.

There was a string of barges along the shore as he looked and then he heard the creak of the rusty door as Echo opened it and the sound of angry dogs barking and running towards them. There were at least ten Rottweiler's, all of which were scarred in some manner with an ear missing or patches of hair gone. She made a gesture towards the hounds that caused them all to calm and then the two of them entered. All of hounds sat as the two immortals passed and then she lead Elias upstairs and down a long hallway until they reached a large open area.

In it were stacks of books by the thousands, pieces of artwork, paintings and statues from every time period. Everywhere about the room were pots of jasmine, some of them in bushes with bloodless white flowers releasing their fragrance into the night air like a spirit that rises after the sun has set, rising as the waxing moon ascends toward a perfect circle; a full and radiant celestial bloom. Others stretched their vines along the corners of the walls, their shiny oval leaves and tubular, waxy-white flowers glistening beneath the lamps of incandescent light. It intoxicated him.

But, the real inebriant was her. Elias's eyes followed Echo as though the strings of his heart were laced through them and out and into her hands. And she held them taut. No move went unnoticed. Each coil of hair that shifted and fell as she turned was like a silent spell. He watched the light and the shadows play around the curves of her face, her delicate cheeks and the curve of her brow and in the recesses, where the shadow turned the eye wells into pools of India ink, two gleans of silver drove out and into him like hooks to draw him nearer. And he moved nearer.

He felt weightless as he went towards her and he could see her pouted lips open, see the rise and fall of her breasts and then his hand was on her waist and her hands were sliding into his jacket and up his chest until they reached his shoulders and then the jacket fell in a blue heap to the floor. Elias pressed his lips softly to hers as the jasmine raced wild in his mind. He kissed her slowly, tasting every part of her lips and her tongue, savoring her as he unbuttoned Echo's coat, each circular one loosed revealing more of the olive flesh beneath, more of the tantalizing skin and then the jacket opened and fell.

A sigh escaped her as Elias's lips moved to her neck and his fingers glided down her back and sides and naked hips. Then he felt her fingers clutch his back. They tore at him until the shirt was lifted up and off and then he looked into her eyes to see them burning for him. And he was in the fire. Her eyes glowed like white hot coals and as he gazed he felt her hand slide down his stomach until it reached the handle of the mirror.

Instinctively, he grabbed her hand, but her eyes and the jasmine overpowered him so that he let her slide the mirror from his pants. He saw her teeth flare as she did this and then she glanced at the back of the Katoptron, at Narcissus looking dreamily at himself and then she kneeled down and lay the looking glass on Elias's shirt.

The Reflection of Elias Dumont

He was in awe of her as the mirror sounded its fit of rage in his ears, but the cruelty of the looking glass fell muted as Echo unbuttoned his pants and slid them down until they rested on the cool tile floor and then he felt her all around him as she took him into her and his fingers glided through her hair like doves through the night sky.

The drowning feeling came back to Elias, as if the world had somehow slowed down, allowing him to see every color, every motion, every nuance of the experience and then he pulled her up to him and gently moved his hands across her face and back into her hair and her glowing eyes locked again on the blue and green of his own and she kissed his wrist while he moved his lips on the edge of her jaw and further until he reached the lobe of her ear and then he suckled as the two of them descended to the floor. All around him was the water of the river and he was slipping down, down where the jasmine was like a dream and further until his mouth grazed the nipple of her breast, down with the swirling current of her fingers on his flesh until he reached the bottom with his face buried in the river's bed. There he tasted the source of love and life.

Elias's hands caressed her thighs as her back arched and then he moved his fingers up her hips until they reached her stomach where the muscles rolled in waves of pleasure. And he continued as the rain streamed down from heaven and beat on the roof and the glass of the windows, he continued until the rush came and flooded his senses. He made love to her then with her breath hot on his face and her eyes lost in the passion, letting a pullulation of crimson tears loose and he tasted them with his tongue.

"Your blood is sweet ambrosia," he moaned.

"Yes," she sighed, her body moving with his in rhythmic undulations. "Yes," and then she stretched her arm until it reached where his pants lie, slipping the knife from the sheath and holding it before Elias's eyes, the silver gleaning and muting as she turned it and then she pressed the tip to her neck until it penetrated her, "I love you," she said, the words spilling from her.

"Yes," Elias chimed as the knife slipped out and his lips surrounded the gash, his body and her blood erupting in one phantasmagorical explosion. And his mind opened to her mind as the blood rushed in, flooding his mouth, filling his body and in his mind's eye he watched the clocks wind down and the earth itself come to a stop.

The heat of Echo's life force raced through him, awakening each cell of his body. He saw the earth open like a great jasmine bud blooming in the celestial darkness, each petal opening to him. There was the beat of her heart pounding against him, pounding as her breasts pushed against his chest, pounding with her legs cleaved to his and her nails digging into his back and then he saw her in the flower as the petals rose into flames. He saw her laughing as the fire spiraled up and over her until it engulfed the image and then it unfolded as a terrible hand, its fingers like whorls of flame. It was the hand of Hades and in its palm was the looking glass.

The sight of it caused Elias to pull away from her. He felt her fingers run down his arm as his body curled into a fetal position on the tiles. There was the sensation of falling down a long spiral, falling, a blood induced vertigo and he shook with the tinny taste of blood in his mouth. Echo's fingers were tiny daggers on his arm, the opaque nails precipitous as they cut along his skin and as he fell further there was the hand looming in his mind, the red burning hand with the Katoptron and then the face appeared and Elias bellowed a long and sorrowful cry.

"Shhh," she whispered, her fingers trailing from his arm and combing through his hair. "It is the blood, Elias. Shhhh. The feeling will pass."

Then he felt it. As the rust in his veins became fluid again, he felt it. With a slow painful thud his heart awoke again. He clutched his chest and gasped. "Echo," but then another pang came stronger than the first, the atrophied muscle pushing the sludge through his body as it changed. Then another pang was there, the pain strung through his body as if something were working a fish stringer about his innards, lacing the chord through every muscle and tendon.

"You are alive again, my love," she said, a crystal phoenix glowing in her irises. "You are alive again."

With every beat his body grew stronger, the blood more fluid. There was a tearing in his gums as the canine teeth were pushed out, as the new roots took hold and the fangs sprouted towards the back of his throat. They were milky white and soft when he touched them. Then another sensation came, but this was one he understood. It was the sluggish feeling of being too intoxicated. It caused his eyes to grow heavy.

"You're tired," she said. "Come. The day will break soon and we need our rest. There is a whole new world that awaits you tomorrow."

"I am really alive," he uttered as he took her hand.

"Yes," she assured him, bringing his body closer to hers and kissing him.

"I am so very tired."

"As am I," she said. "I am weak with the blood loss. Come."

She led him then to a corner of the room where the flowers grew up along the wall and there a beautiful coffin lay open. It was made of snakewood and on it was a rich lacquer that brought out the tones and patterns in the wood. He marveled at the textures of it for a moment and then she placed her hand gently on his back and kissed him and moved him to lie on the white silk that lined the bedding. Then, in a fluid motion, she slipped her naked body in with his, pressing against his flesh as he held her, her neck turned for a final kiss and then the lid to the coffin closed and the darkness fell like a kiss from Azrael, his angelic wings covering them as Elias's heart beat steady against Echo's perfect skin and in the darkness his eyes closed and the world fell into a silent oblivion.

Chapter 10

In the misty gray of the morning, Videl stood in the road. He stood there like some hellish raven, menacing and elongated and he stood there eyeing the naked lot of stained concrete with its myriad of cracks that seemed to vein out and towards him from the abandoned building. There was a hunger in his coruscant eyes that would just show when the wind cut across the brim of his smooth black stove pipe hat, but he was patient. He knew the carrion was going nowhere.

Behind him were three of the five hired men Videl had brought with him. They were a scabby lot, addicts mostly, desperate for a quick buck and the next fix. Each of them was defiled with mud and two of them smoked nervously while the third shivered with something more than cold. The one shivering was in a t-shirt browned with the soil of the earth and it clung to his meatless ribs as the mist continued to descend like a plague upon the land. On his chest a mold could be seen growing also, which flowered up and around his collar in a green ring. It fed on him as any of the other parasites did that infested his body and his surroundings.

"Here comes Bigs," One of the smoking men said and then he coughed and spat from his gray and rotting teeth.

Videl eyed the men with his peripheral and then turned again to the lot. He could see Bigs coming at a quick pace, his head turning occasionally to check for the thing he was cursing at. The other men kept alternating their view from Bigs to Videl with a growing concern for the job they had signed onto. It was clear that something had gone terribly wrong as Bigs was by name and reputation, just that, big and not someone who could be easily rattled and when he reached the road the men looked with astonishment and fear as Bigs pointed a bloodied mangled hand at Videl.

"Mother fucker," he bellowed as he sucked air into his massive lungs. "Did you know there was fucking dogs in there?"

"I had a feeling"

"You had a feeling? Crazy fucked up son of a bitch. Them dogs kilt Darius. He went through the door in front of me and they tore that mother fucker apart, tore his limbs right the fuck off."

"Then it's a good thing Darius went first."

"Bitch, I ought a break your neck."

"You need to shut your god damned trap," Videl said, pulling the shotgun from his trench coat and placing the barrel in Bigs face. "Now go to the van and get the duffle bag."

Bigs pushed the shotgun away from his face and glared, his hand glossy with blood as it ran from the tears and toothed puncture wounds and then he turned, walking between the two smoking men who sensibly stepped aside, and went to the van and opened the back door. He was mumbling and cursing under his breath as he came back and when he reached them he dropped the duffle bag on the street.

Tobias spat again through his rotting teeth and then he pitched his cigarette and bent to one knee,

The Reflection of Elias Dumont

unzipping the bag. In it was a box of stud nails, 16 penny stainless, two hammers, some heavy rope and five new Coleman machetes, still in the box. He looked at the other three men and then he looked at Videl who was sliding the gun back into his coat and then he pulled four machetes out and stood up and gave each man a box.

They set about tearing the boxes open, the cardboard and plastic falling on the wet ground, some of them tumbling and clicking to the curb as they went. The nervous man looked out of sorts as he held the blade in his hands. He had the look of a tattered slave who, after being starved, was handed a weapon and thrown into the Roman colosseum for some sort of sacrificial blood sport. The eighteen inch blade quivered as he trembled.

"The overcast has me concerned," Videl said to the men as he pulled his own blade from its sheath. "We will need to act fast when we get inside. Do not falter. Every last dog must be killed. When this is finished, move quickly upstairs. There you will find a coffin. Go straight to it. Do not touch anything until the coffin is nailed shut. Do I make myself clear?" he growled, his voice low and urgent as he pierced them with his eyes. "When the coffin is secured then the spoils are yours."

As Videl spoke his body seemed to arch and with the long blade in his hand he had the look of a mad grim reaper or some sinister clown come from a circus born out of the bowels of hell. Tobias looked at him as the others began to move towards the building, he looked at the intransigent visage as he knelt again and zipped the bag and then Videl looked at him, his eyes like two spears bent on impaling the man and then he nodded, keeping his terrible gaze upon Tobias as what appeared to be small worms moved silently across the white sclera of one of Videl's eyeballs. His blood ran cold and he had the sudden mortifying notion that he had sold his soul to the devil as he placed the bags straps over his shoulders and then he shivered so that it broke his gaze and with his head down he began to march to the building as well.

Videl filed in beside him as they walked across the void and puddle ridden lot. He walked with long deliberate strides as the argonaut hunched forward. He didn't look at the man, he just walked and when they were nearly a quarter of the way through the lot he asked Tobias, "Do you know what I find curious about man?"

"No," the man said, turning his head away and pressing a stream of spit out of his teeth with a hiss.

"What I find curious is that they have never changed. With all of their so called advancements, the volumes of history they have amassed and all of their leaps in technology they have not changed. They are the same as the day their hairless ape ancestors left the tree and set out upon the land. They are the same."

"You talk about people like you ain't one."

"So."

"So, are you? Human."

"What do you think?

Tobias hiked the bag higher to his shoulders and then he looked at Videl. "I think your Satan mister."

Videl laughed as he said this and then shifted his eyes to him as they walked, twirling his knife in his hand as a drummer might a drumstick. "I am no Satan, nor have I encountered such a thing or seen the fires of hell or any form of brimstone, but if I did I would call him brother for in this world there is no such thing as evil or good for that matter, there is only nature and each thing on this earth acts according to its nature. The idea of good and evil is a man made invention, a farce built into society with the vain inclination of creating order. But, it runs deeper than this for if you look into the guts of it and truly expose good and evil for the fraud they are, you will find they are a sham put forth by the weak and powerless of the world in order to protect them from those who would exert their will over them. The very idea of it runs counter to natural law."

"And what's natural law?" he said as he lit another cigarette.

"The strong survive and the weak die."

Tobias felt another chill as he said this and when they reached the back of the building they could hear the growl of the dogs inside. The hounds emitted a low rumbling sound that echoed in the darkness of the empty space and as Bigs opened the rusty door two dogs came through an open window and charged them.

The nervous man swung wildly at them as they came, his machete taking the ear of one of them, but it did not seem to faze it. Instead the beast raged with its viscous teeth ripping at the man's flesh and then the other dog was on him and he was hacking blindly.

Tobias let the bag slip from his shoulders and then he swung. The blade of the machete swept across the back of the dog's neck as it hung like a great leach from the bloody mans arm. The cut severed the spine causing its massive body to go limp, but the jaws remained clamped. The wiry man let out a cry as his blade tumbled out of his hands and then he fell with the weight of the animals, the second one going for his throat as Tobias brought the blade down again and split its muzzle through.

The hound whelped and then it tried to snap its discerped snout and jaw, but the second swing chopped into its skull with a dull thudding sound and the dog fell over. The other men had left Tobias to his fate and charged inside, leaving him with his heart pounding fiercely in his ears as he tried to catch his breath. He took a long draw of air into his nose and then he looked at the ragged man on the ground, his blood pooling with the water about him and he lay dead, the paralyzed hound still growling, with the blood hissing from its mouth. He placed a foot on the dead dogs face and worked the machete back and forth until it came loose from the skull and then he squared himself and chopped until the other dog had gone silent and cold as well.

He thought about how insane this all was, that he had just killed two dogs with a machete and that two of the men that came here with him were dead as well and he looked over at the bag that lie soaking on the ground, the strange contents within it, nails for a coffin and then he turned and stepped towards the door where the sounds of men wailing and dogs growling came and there was the sound of clothing ripping and of hacking

The Reflection of Elias Dumont

and then the man stepped through the doorway. The light was poor at best and when Tobias stepped in his foot slipped in what he realized was a slick of blood. To the immediate left of the door lay one of the great Rottweiler's, a mutant thing larger than any Rottweiler he had ever seen and he had seen many at the dog fights.

It took his eyes a moment to focus and as he looked he saw what appeared to be the silhouette or shadow of Videl moving about the room, his great blade slashing in a macabre kind of dance. His stove pipe hat appeared taller. Everything about the madman did. But, he was in his element as he cut and spun and gashed, his nature was this, this dark ballet of death. Then he heard the thwack of another blade as it struck the rib cage of some other dog. The creature let out a curdling howl that grabbed Tobias's attention and there in a desperate corner was the silver glean of Bigs' machete.

The behemoth brought the long blade down in a violent swipe, but the blade was all he could see save the glinting of the dog's eyes. There was nearly a complete absence of light in that dismal corner and as he moved closer he realized the other man that had been smoking with him was on the ground and that Bigs was attempting to save him. There were four hounds unlacing the fallen man though, his face mutilated like a raw piece of meat that had been beaten with a tenderizer and as Tobias brought his blade across the neck of the dog it released and spun with a vicious flaring of its teeth.

A second dog left the man's leg and turned on Tobias also. He tried to finish the first hound instead of worrying about the second and so he swung and as he did this the second dog lunged. His machete cut across the open mouth of the first dog, shaving off its top teeth as it passed, slicing the inner part of its throat. It let a gurgled whine and rolled its head to one side on the ground, its paws clicking and scratching on the concrete floor, but the second dog had made its mark.

The hounds solid head bore into his chest as it came snarling and the force took Tobias off his feet. He made a blind roll as he hit the floor and as he did this the dogs hot breath needled his shoulder blade, the Rottweiler gnawing as it tried to sink its teeth. He just kept rolling. He rolled until he struck the wall and with the grit and the stones all stuck in his elbow he swung. The blade made a loud dull thud against the side of the dog which sent it shifting to the side and he felt the cheap plastic handle of the machete break and pinch his palm.

He tried to grasp it again tightly but the dog's paws were pressed into his abdomen and it was looking him in the eyes like something possessed of a thousand ravenous souls, with its teeth flared and the drool slopping from the corners of its mouth and its godless throaty growl rattling towards his throat and then a blade sank into its skull.

Tobias's chest heaved and he had certainly pissed himself as he sat trembling and then the dog slumped over. He looked up to find Videl standing over him and he was standing with that swagger that came with utter confidence. His hat seemed twice as tall from his seat on the floor and as Tobias looked at him he made a

The Reflection of Elias Dumont

gesture to the brim of his hat and dipped his head slightly.

"Go get the bag son," Videl said merrily. "We've got some work ahead of us." Then the dark figure made a jerk and heaved his blade from the carcass and turned and whistled and walked away.

"That was some fucked up shit," Bigs said as he walked up beside him and stood with his yellowish eyes looking down on him.

Tobias said nothing as he brought his legs up and pushed off the wall and stood. He ran the back of his hand along his nose and sniffed and then he spat into the darkness. Bigs just stood looking around as if the dead hounds might rise and attack them again. He looked towards the door and saw the rain coming down through the open window, then he brushed the bits of rock and broken glass from his arms and his pants and picked the broken machete up and walked away to get the bag.

When walked back in Bigs was standing by the door waiting for him. He was shaking his massive hand for the pain and so Tobias paused and drew out his cigarettes from his pants and donned two of them, placing both in his mouth and then he lit them and gave the man one. Bigs took the smoke and gestured a thank you. He did this as men will often do, speaking with no words, nothing but the simplest of motions and then the two of them ascended the stairs.

When they reached the top floor and entered the great room they found Videl sitting on the coffin. He had torn down the heavy drapes that covered the windows, this allowing the filtered light of the gray and overcast sky into the room and as Tobias sat the bag down he noticed something wholly different about Videl. He wore a faint grin upon his face, but the face was now that of a young man, younger than even him. He had his gloves off as well and in his eyes was a shimmer as if the devil had been letting tears of joy.

"Bring the hammers and nails, quickly," Videl motioned.

Bigs took a hammer from Tobias, but he had noticed the change also and so he stood terrified with the cigarette jutting from his mouth and the smoke twisting from it like a gray band of party streamers towards the ceiling.

"Come on," Tobias urged. "Let's get this done."

Bigs moved with him to the coffin and they began nailing the lid shut. They nailed with all urgency and panic and as they drove the nails they began to hear a pounding in the box and a scratching. Videl had placed one leg over his knee and twisting his body had laid one hand as a brace upon the lid and as the clawing in the coffin became louder he began to laugh. The two men just kept to their work until the entire outer rim had been nailed securely and then they backed away. Bigs kept looking at Tobias and then back to the coffin, his yellowed eyes bugging as he tried to rationalize the madness of it. Tobias just stood with his eyes narrowed, his cigarette still dangling from his mouth as he watched the madman gloat over his victims.

"You should have never brought him here," Videl said to Echo. "It was the Katoptron that led me here, to your layer; the Katoptron that gave away your whereabouts." He slid down from the coffin as he said this and then he slapped the lid with the palm of his hand and placed and ear to the lacquered wood.

In the coffin he heard the faint and muted voice of Echo, but then his eyes widened and he stood upright like a man who had just struck upon a fabulous idea or like an old plebian that had just been told they'd won the lottery. Videl cupped his hands together in a celebratory fashion then, looking at the two men who stood awestruck with every manner of bewilderment and fear and then he placed his hands outspread upon the casket and began to laugh.

"You're in there with her," Videl crowed. "You're both in the box together. This is precious."

He turned to the two men again with the look of a demonic school boy just given his first kiss and then he told them to start moving the antiquities, that anything they carried out was theirs, but the coffin. The coffin, he said, was for the hole they had dug in the earth and then he told Bigs to fetch the van around. The man was grateful to leave his bizarre company and he could see the worry in Tobias's eyes as he glanced to him and then exited the room. Tobias said nothing. What was there to say, but that he had indeed sold his soul, but to something far worse than the devil himself.

Videl had turned again and slapping the coffin said, "You know, Elias, I thought you were smarter than this." He then sniggered and trundled his fingers about his lips. "Yes, I thought you were better than this and quite honestly you have been a formidable adversary, the most impressive of them all in fact, but in the end you let your dick get you caught. It's laughable really but then, isn't that how the Roman almost got you also?

Soon you'll know the dirt Elias. You'll know the dirt as I knew the dirt, the foul suffocation of its darkness and the communion you will hold with its decomposers. But don't worry. I will visit your plot on occasion and on the holidays I will adorn it with a wreath and who knows, maybe I'll even plant a tree atop it."

It took the three of them nearly four hours to drag the contents of that room down and out and into the white box van and once they were finished they climbed into the cab with the blood and the sweat about them and they drove away. It was still raining and Tobias sat focusing on the windshield wiper, its whine as it ran its rubber squeegee across the glass in its timed and hypnotic manner. It had the melancholy of a purgatorial sentence. All Tobias could think about was the coffin and that in it were two people who were alive and that he was going to bury them alive for if he didn't he would certainly die himself and be buried right along with them.

Part of him worried this may happen one way or the other. It frightened Tobias to think of Videl, his inhuman qualities, the worms that seemed to be swimming within his face, his body; the man's ease of movement through the darkness as he slew the hounds and his transformation. What in that room had changed him, healed him, delivered that demon from his miserable form. Tobias sat now beside him with a shiver walking up his spine.

The Reflection of Elias Dumont

He pulled his eyes away from the mechanical motion of the wipers, from their ordered and logical rhythm and then he looked at his own shirt stained in shades of brown from the mud and dirt and the spatters of blood that soaked and spread on the wet cotton in a barbarous tie-die fashion. He was stained in chaos. Videl sat motionless against the passenger side door, his hat plugged atop his knee and his hand resting on something beneath his shirt. Bigs was silent as well, his mauled hand resting across his lap as he drove them over the river Des Peres.

As Tobias looked out and over the bridge he could see the groups of people working feverishly to sandbag the levees with the water skimming ever closer to the tops of the man made barriers. The river looked like a vast aqua-duct as if the water was running on a suspension above the channel and horizon of the houses and buildings along its borders, but in truth it was a deep and destructive serpent that pressed and pushed at the skin that contained it.

They drove until they reached a dirt road potted heavily from the rain and they continued down it until they could see the Mississippi river running parallel to the passenger side of the van and then they came to the spot where they had dug the grave. The van lurched to a stop and then Bigs proceeded to turn it and back it up to the spot where a piece of plywood and some sandbags covered the hole. They had stolen the sandbags the day before from the very levee they had passed to get here and as they got out of the van Tobias looked at them ominously and then began to pitch the water logged bags off. When he was finished Videl flipped the plywood over and exposed the hole, which had filled considerably with water.

Bigs had gone to the back of the van, unlatching the door and trundling it up and then he grabbed the shovels with a clang and threw them onto the muddy ground. Next he slid a ramp out and hooked it to the back of the van and let the end of it drop into the watery grave. It made a terrible splash and before it had stopped teetering Videl had launched himself upon it and climbed into the van.

"Quickly now," Videl urged. "We mustn't be spotted." Then he pressed himself against the foot of the coffin. "Au revoir, Elias Dumont," he said, but there was no response. The two lamias lay frozen in that cell together; the full of the day upon them, the rigormortis that it induced and then Videl pushed and slid the coffin forward.

The other two men grabbed at the sides of it as the head of it emerged from the van. It only took one good heave for the ramp was wet and the wood was slick and so the beautiful box went plummeting down. The sarcophagus went like a freakish bob sled, rattling slightly on the ridges of the ramp and then it crashed into the muddy water with the corner of the coffin being wedged into the soft earth at the head of the grave.

Bigs then stood up with his chest heaving and as he turned he found Videl was already upon him. He was close enough to kiss him with his immortal eyes locked to his, refracting the gray light like the cells of water falling around them and there in that closeness Bigs's own eyes dimmed as the life coiled out of them and then Videl pulled the great knife out of the man's chest.

The Reflection of Elias Dumont

It made a sucking noise and then the brute slumped over and fell with a thud atop the coffin.

"Shit. Shit," Tobias yelled as he paced about. "Why did you have to stick him?"

"He was going to try and kill me, Tobias," Videl said, tossing the man a shovel. "He had to be dealt with." With that he turned and went to the door of the van and got in and then he pulled the van forward, allowing the coffin and Bigs to fall completely into the grave and then leaving the van running he got out and picked a shovel up.

Tobias stood lighting a cigarette with the shovels handle wedged into his arm pit. He was trembling and cursing as he did this and when he got the cigarette lit he took a long draw and then he looked grievously into the hole. Bigs lay staring into the rain, his arms outstretched and his neck unnaturally bent. The blood was bubbling from his chest and one of his legs was off the edge of the coffin, partially submerged in the murky water. He realized as he looked at him that Bigs was not dead and as Videl pitched a shovel full of dirt upon him that question that fills the dying's eyes filled his and then Tobias began to shovel as well.

Chapter 11

On August 1st an additional two and a half feet of water spilled into the river Des Peres from the onslaught of rain that over bore the Missouri river. The widespread flooding caused large propane tanks to come loose from their moorings and float away. Entire communities were evacuated as the waters filled their homes and churches and businesses. Graveyards that flooded became supersaturated and in the soft earth the airtight coffins rose like nightmare bobbers on a lake of mud and soot and debris.

For many it seemed the end of days was upon them and as the coffins drifted it would have seemed that Christ had returned and delivered those dead like an army of waterlogged Lazarus's from the tomb. A maniacal parade of god's chosen. They drifted newly dead and long dead alike until the small boats that ferried them were fished out and stored until they could one day be laid again in their plot of eternal slumber.

Along the River des Peres a fifteen foot section of the levee had also burst open. The dark brown water poured through the mouth of that break and filled a long strip of Alabama Ave. Homes were flooded, businesses destroyed, much of which was unsalvageable. Entire neighborhoods were lost or historical sites nearly as old as Elias was himself. He could smell the river also. Elias could smell it and even taste it as it saturated the coffin and he knew what was coming. Echo, on the other hand, was going mad.

She had clawed for days at the lid of the casket, shredding the silk lining and splintering the thick wood, but Elias had laid calm against her, his naked skin against her skin as the nights came and they awoke to the darkness. He was weak also. Neither of them had fed for several days and in their earthen prison had grown frail and leathery. Today though he could smell the river as the ground swelled and the River des Peres backed up where it met the force of the mighty Mississippi and above them the water crested and deepened until the soil became so loose that it could not hold the contents in its possession and they rose.

Like a pair of submariners they came to the surface, the odd vessel popping up and slapping the water as a whale might do upon the sea and then they drifted. It was still day, mid afternoon as the couple churned in the treacherous current, colliding with debris as the coffin went in its missile form until finally it struck, what use to be a large pole barn and drifted into a sparsely flooded wood.

They eddied in this place until the sun sank and that corner of the earth joined them in darkness and then the two of them awoke. They awoke with a thirst and a vengeance in their hearts. Elias struck first at the lid of the coffin. His newly formed fangs jutted from his mouth as he hissed and then he struck again, but this time as he hit she hit as well. It caused the lid of the coffin to crack and pop, the coffin bobbing in the shallow water, bobbing from the swaying of their working bodies. Each strike brought a higher pitch with it, their minds working under the spell of a singular thought and then the nails whined and groaned and the blue light of the evening darkness peaked in.

The sight of freedom caused them to strike harder and faster and each one brought the lid higher until it flung away and landed with a crash in the soup like water. The two of them looked alien as they stepped naked from the pod that held them, their bodies emaciated and pale like the faint sliver of moon that crept through the dark clouds. They slithered through this dark and flooded wood with only the sound of the water rippling around the groaning trees. There were no birds or deer or any other living thing for that matter, nothing save these lost souls until they reached a muddy elevation on the plain. There, at the edge of the tree line, a group of large black birds roosted in the limbs.

One of the great birds roused, its wings stretching as the two of them hunched and looked about in the open. It cawed at them as Elias looked at it and then one after another began to caw as well, each one in rapid succession until the entire group was in an uproar. He turned to them and stood upright and then like the very water, Echo moved, her liquid motion so quick the birds did not detect her until she had scaled the tree and had one in her teeth. It caused a panic amongst the others. Each one stretched their immense wings and broke into the navy sky. They looked like a great shifting tare in the fabric of space and time and then they drifted across the scant light of the grinning moon and were gone.

Elias stood watching her as she fed, the dark creature slack in her hands as she crouched like some gargoyle atop a gothic cathedral. She was only in her perch for a matter of minutes, but Elias took it all in, the shades of blue black in the silent sky and the light wind that brought the smell of the dank and open flood plain.

He heard the crash of the dead bird as it met the grass and the mud on the ground and then she was beside him again. Her eyes were radiant. They were the only thing that didn't seem to have a bluish hue to them and he marveled at them as she pressed in close.

"You must feed," she said, kissing his bottom lip as he held her to him. "Come. There are morsels in this direction," her eyes looking west across the open fields.

"How do you know this?"

"Once you have fed your senses will heighten," she smiled.

"And even the bird has awakened these senses in you?"

"Yes."

"I can see the color returning to your skin," he said, running the back of his fingers down her cheek. "I never knew you could move so fast."

"Yes," she said. "And you can move this way as well. The laws that governed you in your life govern you no more. Come," she said again. "Keep up with me. Let your mind open and let your body do what comes natural to it."

He followed her then across the open country, the soggy ground where great patches of mud slicked the earth, cutting through the air and the tall grass as he pursued her naked body, the long hair that coiled away from her like black smoke in the darkness. He watched the muscles in her pale form flex with supple ripples as she ran effortlessly and he was exhilarated by this and by all of his own new possibilities. Elias had known power with the looking glass, had felt unstoppable at times, but that power was dwarfed now by this new magic. He was a cherub turned archangel. The speed in which they moved astounded him and how they barely seemed to touch the ground, the grass and the weeds swishing as they passed as though the breeze had simply swayed their stalks and leaves and then allowed them to fall back into place.

He followed Echo in this way until they reached an old barn atop a bluff. The barn was lagging in the center of its vaulted roof and it had the look of an old and mistreated mule, a mule with a swayed back and one foot in the ground. Elias looked up at the silent and aging piece of Americana with its gray boards and black hollows where the joints had buckled and opened and the wood had shifted, bowed, broke and splintered. At his feet were pieces of the roof that had come down and he bent and picked up a small plank. It had a torn and curled strip of shingle on it and he looked at it inquisitively for a moment and then tossed it away. The chunk landed with a flop in the wet weeds and then Elias stood, clapping the dirt from his hands and then he turned and looked out across the flood plain.

In the distance he could see the shimmer of the moon light stretch across the inundated American Bottom flood plain. For miles there was nothing but silt rich water that now ran where the corn and wheat and the soy had grown. Roofs peaked out of the water in spots, barely noticeable in the far off shadows of muck and shifting flow. Echo touched him as he gazed out, her fingers like silk ribbons on his shoulder and as he turned his head to her the delicate tips slid down his arm and into his hand.

The Reflection of Elias Dumont

"Breathe in," she spoke softly. "Do you smell the morsels?"

He let the air wash through him, the smells flooding his senses and then he caught it. The smell was faint at first, but as he narrowed his focus, it became a singular portentous smell. She led him by the hand around the barn and when they reached the edge of the infirm structure he could see the house. There was a light on over the back porch. It illuminated the weathered decking with its peeling paint and with his reborn eyes he could see the insects that flew like kamikazes around the incandescent lamp, all of them eager to die like their kin whose husks lie in small heaps upon the base of the glass dome.

The domicile itself was an old two story farm house. Not a board on the home remained true as gravity and settling had plagued it and it too was peeling the many layers of paint so that it looked like a diseased birch tree whose bark was curling from its trunk. He stood there eying these things until he heard the sliding door open and then a hand slid the screen door as it scratched unevenly in its track and then an old man stepped out and slid the screen closed behind him, shooing the moths that fluttered about his head and then he stepped forward and turned so that he was facing the barn and the yard and the two lamias that stood in the baleful shadow.

The old man then pulled a black pipe from his back pocket and placed it in his mouth where it stood a stark contrast against the silver hairs of his well groomed beard. Elias could smell the tobacco as he lit it and he could smell the man's cologne and the sweat of his day, but most of all he could smell his blood. Elias wanted to move and take him then, but Echo stayed him.

"Excuse me, sir," She said, her voice timid as she covered her private areas with her arms and hands and stepped forward.

"Who is that?" the man said, dropping his pipe. "Who's there?"

"My name is Echo," she answered, stepping further out so that the old man could see her. "And this is my husband Elias. We were swept down river by the flood."

The man squinted at them, "Dear lord," he declared, his eyes popping open as he turned and went to the door. "May! May! Come here, honey," he yelled as he slid the screen door open and went inside. In a moment he returned and in his hands were two crocheted afghans. "Come on up to the house," he said as the old man went down the steps of the porch. "Are either of you hurt?"

"No," Elias said. "But we've lost everything."

"It would appear so," the old man said grinning. Then he handed Elias an afghan and turned and let the second one drape from his hands so that he could wrap it around Echo. She thanked him as he did this and he assured her it was nothing.

On the porch the old man's wife, May, had come out and she was fretting at them to come inside as she adjusted and tightened the belt of her robe. She had the irrepressible look of beauty that neither age nor the recent awakening from sleep could detract. This was

The Reflection of Elias Dumont

something Elias perceived immediately as he ascended the three wooden steps of the back porch. He thanked her for helping them as his eyes fell in a gated sort of lust upon her and it was such that the woman began to blush with an innocence she had not felt since her childhood.

"You poor dears," May said with a smile that brimmed from one rosy cheek to the other. "You come inside and get cleaned up and I'll try and find some cloths for you."

Echo thanked her warmly as she stepped between May and Elias's gaze, his eyes shimmering like emeralds under the porch light. "We've been walking for hours and this is the first house we've come upon," Echo pined, shooting a look at Elias as if to tell him to be in more control and then they went into the house.

The old man introduced himself as Walter and then he proceeded to ask them how they had been swept away by the river. He wanted to know all about their ordeal, what it was like when the flood came and then he kept repeating that he just couldn't imagine such a terrible thing.

"Well," Elias began. "My wife and I are from the Carondolet area of St. Louis. We had a small house up there not far from the river Des Peres. Echo and I were just getting ready to take a shower when the water came." Elias pulled the afghan tighter to him and then he looked at Walter directly. "I tell you sir it sounded like a freight train was coming for the house and then the water rushed in all around us."

"Dear lord," May said from the kitchen as she poured water into a coffee maker and closed the lid. "You all must have been scared to death."

"I know I was," Echo said. "My husband stayed pretty calm though. He's the one who thought of climbing out the window and up the antenna to the roof."

"Yes," Elias continued. "If we hadn't gone up on the roof I don't think we'd be here talking to you right now." Elias went to Echo then and stood close beside her as May came out of the kitchen and the coffee ran into the pot.

"What did that house up and float off on you," Walter remarked as he pulled a handkerchief from his pocket and blew his nose, wiping the hanky from side to side before folding it over and placing it back in his pocket.

"Yes. Yes, sir. We weren't on the roof more than five or ten minutes before it started to groan and buckle, next thing we knew we were out in the middle of what looked like a lake and there were all matter of things floating down the river with us. Hell," Elias said. "There was even a coffin that went floating by."

May gasped when he said this, making the sign of the cross with her hand.

"Well, you kids are real lucky to be alive," Walter said smiling. "Our son Bill is a volunteer fireman. He left this morning to help move those folks from the village Valmeyer to higher elevation. He said the whole village is lost."

"I'm gonna go find some cloths for the both of you," May said. "The bathroom is right around the corner there if the two of you want to take a shower and get that mud off yah. Towels are under the sink. Just help yourself."

"We appreciate you being so kind to us," Elias said and he nodded to Walter as he and Echo turned and walked down the hall.

"Here," May called to them as she leaned against the rail of the stairs. "Let me find you some clothes before you get in the shower." Then she turned and went up to the second floor where the bedrooms were.

They could hear her fretting as she looked through the drawers, her sweet voice as she spoke to herself, no, no, that won't fit and the sound of the wood slapping shut. She was gone less than five minutes when she came down holding an old blouse with a large floral print on it and a pair of black slacks and beneath it was a pair of blue jeans and a long sleeve cowboy style shirt that had a light blue and green plaid on it and pearl buttons on the cuffs and the pockets and all up the front as well. She walked passed them and sat the clothes on the sink in the bathroom and the couple thanked her warmly again.

"The slacks might be a bit short on you dear," May said smiling. "But the waist should fit you fine. Those pants are going to be a little big on you though," she directed at Elias. "My Bill is a might stockier than you are, but it will get you through."

"When you kids get out of the shower you're welcome to the phone too," Walter chimed in, his hands in his pockets as he motioned with his head at the phone on the wall. "I recon your family thinks the worst."

"Yes sir," Elias said with a nod and then the two stepped into the bathroom and closed the door.

Echo turned the overhead fan on for noise and then she bent and pulled two towels out from beneath the sink and closed the honey oak veneered door and sat the towels on top of the clothes. Then they let the afghan's drop to the floor, which, Elias proceeded to bunch into the corner with his muddy foot until they were one piled on top of the other in a heap and he turned and saw Echo's naked body bent over the tub to start the water. There was the squeak of the knobs as she turned them and the rush of the water as Elias smoothed his hands across the mud stained skin of her back. Then he let his hands drift down and over her buttocks and on to her thighs and then back up and as he did this she flipped her long hair over to one side and looked at him with a seductive smile, pulling the stopper up so that the shower engaged and the hot water came streaming down in its pattering against the sea foam green ceramic tub.

She stood up then and stepped into the tub, the water spraying and streaming down her olive skin as the brown mud ran from her feet, thinning to something almost clear before it coiled down the drain. Elias stepped in too. He placed his cold hands on her warm flesh and it stirred him and then she pressed herself against him and felt the excitement of him, felt the throbbing of the muscle as the blood and the beat of his heart pulsed and then he was joined to her.

The Reflection of Elias Dumont

Her fangs, two ivory daggers, came forward as she opened her mouth with her head arched back and the hot water gushing tirelessly down as they moved in synchronous vacillations. He swept the long wet strands of hair from her neck so that it all flowed over her right shoulder and then he kissed the exposed nape with the water trailing around his lips and the taste of her flooding his thoughts.

When they had finished showering they put the clothes on and Echo kissed him and then she explained that they must be careful not to kill the morsels. She explained that Elias must use that instinctual thaumaturgy that all lamias posses, that power that he had inadvertently evoked on the porch with his eyes shimmering and his voice hypnotic so that he may put the old woman under his spell. She said then he could taste. But she stressed that he must only taste and that he must not kill her for each kill that could not be concealed is another confirmation of our existence. Echo also warned him that they were not in the safety of their own hunting grounds, that they had no coffin in which to retreat to when the sun rose, no place to hide them from the burning rays and that they could not afford to be pursued.

He asked her about the fang marks and wouldn't the old couple know they were fed upon. She smiled when he said this. Then Echo explained the art of covering ones tracks. She said to only imbibe a small amount, "Un peu," she smiled, enough to leave them sleepy in their trance and when your fangs have left the morsel then to prick your finger and press your blood to the wound so that it may heal them over. But, Elias was still unsure about this, about his own ability to stop, to leave the blood he craved and spoke softly about how he had seen her in that blood lust when she could not stop herself and how her imbibing had appeared to be uncontrollable madness.

"Yes," she said, putting her fingers on his lips. "Too much will do this, will swoon you, will make you mad with it and you will taste until the morsel is dry and the heart has quit and you are blind with only the sound of your own heart beating upon the drums of your ears. It is also a state of bliss, a Shangri-La that you will know someday, but for now," she paused and kissed his lips, "taste."

"And I'll know when to stop?"

"You will know by the resonance of the hearts. When the sound of your heartbeat overtakes the sound of theirs, you must stop."

Chapter 12

It was just after midnight when they left the old couple sitting on the couch like two drunkards. They were snoring heavily and Echo had found a blanket beside the couch and placed it over May and then they had turned the television on and Elias opened the T.V. guide to the back where Walter had been working on the crossword and he sat this across the man's leg and sat a pen in his lap and then the two stood and marveled at their work for a moment and left. They took the two afghan's with them and a thick brown tarp that Echo had found in the barn and each of them a pair of shoes from the front closet and then they set out north across the fields.

They moved as feathers move in the air, with a weightlessness, as if their bodies could defy gravity, but it was the speed and the fluid motion that kept them planing along the surface. They did this until they came upon a road that ran along the bluff and then they slowed and walked. Ahead of them in the distance were the lights of Columbia, Illinois. The thought of entering the town so close to daybreak unnerved Echo and so she stopped and closed her eyes and breathed. To the east she could smell another farm and as she turned towards it Elias closed his eyes in emulation and breathed until he too could smell the farm.

"It's there, through the trees," Echo motioned with her hand. "We need to find a place to bed down for the day and we can partake in the livestock also."

He followed her then through the wood, taking careful note in his mind as she educated him. There was a way about her as she prowled. She was graceful at all times, moving as the wind would move through the trees, her feet avoiding fallen limbs and jutting roots and then they emerged into the open field again. There were a number of barns and sheds, at least ten buildings altogether and the two of them went stealthily along until they reached a paddock containing half a dozen horses. The smell took Elias back again, back into that life of vanity and insecurity.

"I hate horses," he said with his hand over his mouth and his nose and the afghan bunched in his arms.

"They don't seem to care for you either."

"No?"

"No," she said as she walked down the center of the paddock and the horses stirred in their stalls.

A large brown mare neighed, her teeth flaring as Elias stepped forward. He gave her an indignant look and the horse turned and brought her flank against the gate of her stall. She was a beautiful horse and stood at least sixteen hands tall, her head swaying so that her bulbous eye could follow Echo through the slats of the stall and when Echo reached the gate the mare brought her muzzle against the wood plank and snorted.

The lamia placed her hand on the horse's nose and stroked and then she fixed her eyes upon the horse's eye so that in a matter of seconds she had the mare beguiled. With a faint clanking sound she unbolted the gate to the stall and opened the gate so that it whined slowly as it went and she lay the afghan and the tarp over the top rail of the stall as the mare dipped her head and clapped her right rear hoof on the straw and the

The Reflection of Elias Dumont

manure laden cedar chips that lined the paddock and then the lamia stepped in. The horse looked like a great shadowy statue as she stroked its long neck. If it moved it was only from its great lungs drawing in air as it breathed and then she sank her fangs into the creature so that it looked as though she were kissing the mare with her arms wrapped gently about its neck.

She was not on long before she turned and looked at Elias with the full strength of her eyes, those ancient gems and then she bid him to taste. He was reluctant at first, but then he went and sank his teeth in as well. The horse's heart drummed like a hundred human hearts rapping in unison or stronger and the blood rushed into him and made him one with the mare so that he saw her running in a vast open plain like some glorious Elysian field, unending and he was astride her with the wind streaming through her main and his hair whipping and coiling as the blue sky poured ever out before them. He was in heaven. He heard the sound of his heart in tandem with the mares. Generation after generation of the horse's lineage passed across the eye of his mind and he felt the horse's strength residing in him and then, with a gasp of air, he released her.

"I could see inside the horse's mind," Elias said, "I could see her dreams."

"Yes."

"And I feel as strong as a horse now."

"You are stronger," Echo said and then she pricked the end of her finger and pressed it into the wound on the horse and stepped back, shutting the gate behind her and then she grabbed the afghan and the tarp and turned and walked out of the paddock.

At the back edge of the property, they spent the day in a small shed. It was once a chicken coop, but the weathered building had been closed off for years. Elias had pulled the door loose, the dirt and the sod plowing in front of it as it went. Inside, above the door, was a bee's nest, which the prying had disturbed. It caused a flux of bees to fly about in agitation with the humming sound of their waylaid flight coursing around them. Elias swatted at them at first as Echo laughed but the bees didn't make anything of them and after a few minutes they returned to the hive and then the two of them crawled inside and closed the door.

They laid an afghan down on the dirt and then one over them with the tarp on top, rolling themselves until the tarp was covering every bit of their bodies and then they slept. Dreams filled Elias's mind as he lay with Echo's head resting on his shoulder, her legs intertwined with his and the images playing through his conscience like an old film depicting the brutality of his life. He saw the looking glass again. There was a part of his psyche that tried to reach into that astral plain where dreams are born like stars and touch it. The urge to hold it was immense.

He watched the mirror turn in the black void and each time it rotated he caught a glimpse of something in the glass, but he could not see what it was. The image seemed to flip by too quickly or was it the silvery glare cast as the looking glass came circumvolving about, he couldn't tell, but there was something or someone there.

The Reflection of Elias Dumont

At sun set they rose with the heat of the day still nested heavily in the coop. Elias pulled the tarp up and off their heads and he looked at the rows of nesting boxes and then he kissed Echo and spoke nothing of his dreams. They folded the tarp and the afghan's and then Echo pushed the door open. A rush of cool air was welcomed in and as the bee's flew out in their confusion the two of them emerged and were gone across the field. She led him back the way they had came, down the long bank of woods with its maple trees and bald cypresses and when they had reached the edge of the tree line along the road she stopped and sat upon a birch tree that had leaned over and come to rest in the arms of another tree some fifteen feet or so from it.

"I want to change these clothes," Elias said as he stood next to the unearthed roots that splayed out like petrified tentacles from the birch tree. "And I could use a smoke."

Echo rested like a cat on the tree, her arm supporting her body with her legs lying jogged one over the other down the angel of the trunk. She tilted her head as Elias said this and the long strands of hair fell from her shoulder. "Yes," she smiled. "We can follow the road up this way. There's a town not far from here."

"I'm going to get us something to drive too," Elias said, pushing his hand through his hair as he carved a crescent shape into the ground with the toe of his shoe. "I'm not walking all the way back to St. Louis."

"So you want to go back there?"

"Yes. Don't you?"

"I don't know; I guess. I don't know what good will come of it."

"What good," he laughed, turning from her as he walked to the shoulder of the road. "No good comes from anything I do, Echo." He then squatted and picked up a stone and looked at it as if it had some answer inside of it. "No good will come from any of this," he continued, "whether we stay here now or run away to some new corner of the world or return from whence we came our destinies are intertwined and I see that now." Elias stood up slow and easy with the stone clenched in his fist and then he looked at the cat like woman lying on the tree. "And you know something Echo, you were right."

"About what?" she said as she sat up and her feet fell.

"I am a killer." And then he threw the stone so that it went skittering down the road and into the darkness of the night.

There were no stars in the sky nor was there a moon as they made their way up Bluff Rd. and into the town of Columbia Illinois. On the right of the bluff they saw a small fire burning and as they approached it they found a couple sitting on a blanket beside a small hibachi style grill. Their fire popped and crackled as the yellow and orange flames licked at the darkness and cast its ever shifting glow upon the couple. Their motorcycle rested some five feet from where they sat and attached to the back of it was a tow along.

The man had his legs stretched out and he was drinking a beer and smoking as the woman sat Indian style between the V that his legs formed. She had an animated face that the light of the fire accentuated. Echo watched the woman as she laughed and patted the man's chest, her head dipping and braided pony tail falling over her shoulder as the sound of her voice drifted away like the embers, drifting into a concomitant oblivion from which they would never return.

They left them naked and dead inside the stone walls of Fort Piggott. Elias lit a cigarette as he sat on the motorcycle and smoked. He watched Echo braid the long strands of her own hair, braiding them in the fashion of the morsel and then he thought of the mirror again as the embers glowed in the round tripod grill. He saw it turning again. There was the light flickering like the light of the coals, but this time his mind reached out and brought the looking glass closer so that the image in the mirror became more recognizable and when it reached him it slowed its turn and there in the mirror was the lion.

Elias smoked. His eyes stared deeper into the coals, into the vision, the burning eyes of the lion that gazed back at him like blood red garnets and then the lion roared. In its mouth were two saber like teeth. They were long and ivory and he felt the hair of his body stand as they glistened with their awful radiance; two terrible arches designed with a singular destructive purpose. He shuddered when Echo stepped between him and the fire and then she placed her hand on his shoulder.

"You alright?" she asked, looking into his dilated eyes like a psychiatrist, one pupil larger than the other.

He hissed at her and as he did so he realized that his fangs were presenting themselves. "Yes," he muttered pushing his fingers into his hair. "I," he stuttered as he looked at her in confusion and then she bent and picked his cigarette up from the ground and handed it to him.

"You let the fire put you into a trance," she laughed.

"Yes," he said, pulling a long drag from the smoke.

"Be careful not to fall into such a gaze from which you cannot pull yourself away," she warned. "Such a gaze can lead to a calamitous end."

"I'll keep that in mind," he said and then pulled a final drag from the smoke and pitched it. Then he stood and brought his heal down to start the bike. The motorcycle rumbled as Echo slid onto the back of it and wrapped her arms around Elias and then the bike pulled away with the dirt and the gravel spitting behind it.

She held close to him as the wind rushed passed. They drove north with the myopic headlight splaying luminescence out before them. The Mirror was leading him, but he did not understand fully or know even where he was truly going, he simply understood now that he was the lion, that he was pursuant and that he wanted to kill Videl. Elias was nearly blind with the thought of it. He could have been alone. The world rushed bye, the flooded landscape of the plain as he drove beyond the tips of corn stalks that peaked by the thousands from the surface of the dark water. He plied west taking Interstate 50 across the Jefferson Barracks

Bridge and on and into St. Louis again. A sense of urgency was on him. The looking glass was close and he understood now that great desire that the others must have felt as they longed for it, as it called to them like a demonic homing device.

    The night was still young when Elias brought the motorcycle around the abandoned building where the picked over and rotting dogs lie outside the door. Echo sat on the bike as Elias kicked the stand and dismounted the seat. He pulled the cigarettes from the pocket of the shirt and placed one in his mouth and then he offered one to Echo and she took it. Then he lit hers and his and put the lighter in the pack and put it back in the pocket of the faded denim shirt.

    Echo told him she did not want to go inside. She leaned forward on the bike with the smoke between her fingers and she warned him that Videl could be inside, that there could be a trap for them, but Elias just stood with his eyes narrowed and the cherry of his cigarette blazing red as he drew the oxygen into its harbored flame.

    "He isn't here," he said. "There's nothing here but death." He turned from her then and walked to the door. "I'm gonna get my clothes and my things if they're still here. Do you need anything?"

    "No," she said.

    He looked back as she said this and watched the smoke from her cigarette coil around her and the smoke that trailed in wisps from her lips and he thought for a moment that she looked like a ghost or some seductive otherworldly specter and then she pulled the braid loose from her hair and shook it out so that the hair fell all about her face and he smiled and turned and went inside.

    Elias moved quickly through the death fumes and the darkness where the corpses set strew upon the damp cement and grit. Nothing had been there to witness the carnage save the plethora of rats whose nails scratched and scurried as he passed them and the three raccoons whose eyes glazed out of the darkness as they tried to make sense of him and then went on in their foraging unconcerned. There was something akin about those nocturnal creatures, he thought as he made the stairs and ascended. They were, in their likeness, scavengers of the night and he thought even more of this as he rummaged through the overturned books and dust covers and the curtains that were torn down.

    Most of the relics in the room had been removed though. Anything that may have been valuable had been taken, but in one corner there stood several items still under their covers as though the looters had run out of time or space and then, in a hurry, had quit the place. He found his shirt and denim jacket and pants and he gathered them up and then he looked in the pocket of his pants, pulling out the empty money clip and the hotel key. These items went into the pocket of the jeans he was wearing and then he put the jacket on and his own boots, which he found protruding out from an overturned book case.

    After he tied his boots he stood up and walked over to the corner where the untouched items were and he ran his hand over one of the dust covers until he reached the edge and pulled it so that the piano beneath

The Reflection of Elias Dumont

it was exposed. Its importance was lost to him and it seemed everything Echo had built over the unknown length of her existence had been, in a singular blow, taken from her and he felt a growing pain over his cause of it. Some of the covered pieces were sculptures, Greek he thought as he looked at the smooth marble figures and then he came upon the tall piece that rested against the wall and he pulled the cover so that drifted down like a tangled parachute, gathering at his feet as it came.

It was a mirror. The extravagant piece stood some ten feet tall and all about its edge were intricate wood carvings of nymphs and flowers and leaves. Despite the lack of light he could see the shadowy images of the room reflected in it and then he gasped and reached his hand towards the pane of glass for in the mirror was everything about the room save himself. He pressed the palm of his hand to it, but there was nothing except perhaps the faintest hint of a shadow and then he ran his fingers to the center where a queer and disturbing oval had been cut from the pane.

He stepped back from the mirror as he beheld it. All reason escaped him as he tried to tell himself that it wasn't true, but he could now see that his shadow moved about the floor as he moved, but there was no image of him. "How would she have this," he uttered aloud and then the images came. They swirled and coiled within the mirror like something lost and stricken with pain; like blind animals that could still perceive light. They seemed to be unaware of his presence or of anything, but he knew those images for he had seen them all before. He knew their faces, their names and the history of their lives and they were all there now before him swirling around the hole as if it were a portal that led to Dante's hell. The implication was too much for Elias. It caused his eyes to burn and his fangs to flare from his upper gums and then he rushed forward and grabbed the mirror and swung his body so that the great piece came crashing with a rush of air and dust.

When the mirror struck the floor it sounded like a small bomb went off. The glass with its silver backing exploded about the room sending tiny jagged projectiles throughout the space, each of them shimmering as it went. The rage in him was maddening. How she had been there all along, had known everything about all of them, all of those lost souls of the looking glass and that she had known him, his truths and his darkest secrets long before she had ever revealed herself to him, long before that night beneath the moon and the tree when he had glimpsed her, she had known him.

He clutched a handful of jasmine flowers from the wall where they had been flourishing, their nocturnal petals opened to him and he breathed that intoxicating scent in, the scent of her and then the tears came brick red from the corners of his eyes. When he had calmed himself he wiped his face with his shirt and threw the shirt on the ground and then he lit a cigarette and turned and left.

Outside the air was cooler and as Elias stepped through the door he sucked the oxygen in as though he had been drowning. Echo was still setting on the bike. Her face was stained with her own tears and she was trying to look away from him as he approached the bike. He put the cigarette in his mouth and let his eyes pierce her for a moment and then he pushed the hair out of his face and scratched his head. When she didn't say anything to him he huffed and then he threw his leg over the seat and sat down with his boot resting on the clutch pedal.

"Elias," she began.

"Don't speak to me," he interrupted and then his head fell and his bangs slinked into his face. "I don't want your apologies or explanations," he continued. "All I need to know is do you love me or am I just another piece to add to your twisted collection?"

"I love you," she said, wrapping her arms around his chest, her face pressed against his cold shoulder. "I love you."

Chapter 13

They pulled into the parking lot of the Basilica of St. Louis as it sat in its venerable state beneath the halo of the Gateway Memorial Arch. Elias brought the bike to a stop and kicked the stand down, pushing his hand through his hair as the engine of the bike gave off faint tings of heat. Echo slid off the bike and threw her hair back with a flip and then she tamed it with her hands. She pawed at the wind whipped strands like a feline, grooming herself as she watched the flame from Elias's lighter place a glow upon his face.

"He's close," Elias said, the smoke dangling from his lips as he spoke.

"How do you know?" she asked with a level of doubt in her tone.

"I'm still connected to it," he answered. "I thought the blood freed me from the mirror, but it didn't. I still see the mirror in my mind. The feeling of its presence though it's hard to explain," he continued, pulling the cigarette from his mouth and blowing the smoke down towards the pavement. "I just know I'm closer to it."

She took her gaze from him and looked at the clock on the steeple of the Basilica and then she looked back to him. "It's not too late you know. We can still leave here, forget the mirror and Videl and leave."

He sat smoking.

"We could go to Arizona," she continued, "to Phoenix where the heat of the day carries through the

The Reflection of Elias Dumont

night. Or we could go to Portland Oregon. It would be an adventure. I've never seen the west coast."

"I'm going to go up to my hotel room," he said as if she had not spoken at all. "I want my things out of my room."

"Do not go in there, Elias," she said, her voice soft and low as her arms crossed. "Certainly the police have been there and will be watching the room."

He looked at her hesitantly as she said this. "And why would the police be there?"

"Don't act stupid," she scolded. "I know about that dead thing you kept in your room, Robert. I saw that bellboy in your mind when we were connected."

"They'd have no cause to go in my room," he argued.

"Fool," she said, stepping to him and taking the cigarette from his hand and then sucking on it. "Surely someone smelled that dead rat days ago. It probably stunk to high heaven."

"Well," he hissed. "I'm going. I'll take the stairs up," he contested as he stepped away from the bike. "I have the adjoining room beside it also. It's under a different name." He turned then towards the road and looked up as the wind rustled the leaves of a large tree, a tree that stood rooted at the corner of the interstate and Walnut St. and the entrance to the parking lot and he thought of the first time he had seen Echo standing beneath that tree so long ago. "Are you coming?" he asked, even when he knew she would not.

"No."

"Suit yourself," he said with a malignant tone and then he left her.

Echo waited until he was out of sight and then she left as well. She moved as the wind moved, cutting through the trees that stood beside the Basilica and then out across the open lawn of the park. She saw another woman out running her dog as she cut across, the woman oblivious to her surroundings as she ran with her headphones on, but the dog looked, acknowledged her in that unspoken language that all animals are imbued with and the dog trotted on, out in front of the woman with its leash taut and then Echo was in the trees again. In the air a small bat swooped and flew in its silent pattern just above the surface of the reflection pool and then it was gone into the darkness of the night. Echo moved with this silence, moved beneath the canopy of foliage until it opened and then she walked across the parking lot and down, crossing Washington Ave. until she reached the arched entrance of the Metrolink Station where, just inside, two large pillars rose from her flanks like concrete sentinels. She ran her hand lightly across one of the columns, entering as a phantom might, brushing along in its silent wanderings and she looked above her and into the early vacuous morning where the trains had yet to stir from their slumber and then she ascended the stairs.

On the floor of the platform deep shadows crisscrossed down the concrete terminal, some of them rising up and riding along the metal trashcans and benches. She moved silently along as the cars passed above her, each with a dull throbbing that grew and then faded off as the vehicles, with all varieties of

The Reflection of Elias Dumont

passengers, went one after another across the Eads Bridge, that immensity of arches and steel that stretched so defiantly the swollen Mississippi. She moved like silk would move if it had the breath and the desire to do so and she did this until she reached a dark figure sitting on a bench at the far end of the platform.

"Darling Echo," Videl said, the shadow beneath his stovepipe hat pouring down and around his grin. "I'm glad you've come to your senses love and ditched that toy of yours." He said this with all the confidence of a madman as he sat in his mannequin like pose and stared at her. She could not see his eyes for the depth of the darkness, but she could feel his look. It crawled on her as if the two eggish eyes hidden there in the shadow had hatched legions of new born spiders upon her skin. "I must admit that I am rather impressed you found your way out of the ground so quickly; an underestimation on my behalf. There must be a god that favors you yet."

"Favors?" she grinned, stealing through the shadows until she knelt before him, her arms volute about his crossed legs and the serpentine strands of hair settling along her shoulders and back as her head tilted and her eyes warmed and worked him like an ancient forge. "You know, it could be the way it was before," she lulled, her voice hypnotic as the words fell upon him like petals from a flower.

His lips parted as he exhaled. Fingers eased along his inner thigh, gracing his crotch and back down. Videl reeled as she caressed him. He was lost in it, as if she had a thousand hands and he was lost, lost in the inferno of her eyes, those conjuring irises, an orgy of colors bent on flooding his mind with endorphins, those jubilant toxins of inebriation and self deception. He was lost. He found himself at her mercy as he had in the past, as all who had succumbed to the Katoptron had for it was her dark gift or curse to feed upon the vanity of these men, to punish them for the one who had spurned her love and there that voice was, as ancient as hers as it hissed from the looking glass and then a hand struck Echo across the face.

The blow took her from her knees and sent her sliding down the wood slats and iron rails of the tracks. She came to rest some ten feet from where she had landed on her back and when she looked up she saw Elias standing on the platform pale and motionless, his face riddled with hate as he looked at her. Videl had fallen to his knees beside Elias as the pain of his body changing into that terrible form again gripped him. He knew the torturous infliction of every injury as Echo gathered herself and stood and held the mirror in her hand.

A Thin slice of color bled along the eastern horizon as she turned the looking glass and peered into it. There was nothing. No reflection looked back at her, nothing to show her the truth of her existence and so she pressed the mirror to her chest and turned and began to walk down the tracks. She walked with the Greek revival windows open to her side and a gentle wind coming in from the river that stretched out and into the darkness of some unseen place. When she reached the last of the openings she stopped and stepped onto the ledge.

Elias moved to her as though he were the air, as though he had dematerialized and then rematerialized

The Reflection of Elias Dumont

before her, moving like a temporal shade and there he stood with his head bent and his hair hanging over his face. She clung to the mirror as he did this, the looking glass cleaved to her breast, her hands crossed over it as if this could protect it and then he lifted his head so that his burning eyes met hers.

Echo's head tilted then and that old hallowed question filled her eyes, that question Elias had seen and ever left unanswered. The puzzlement dogged him as his heart beat in his throat, pounding with the very blood she had given him and then he pushed her out. She fell through the large archway and as she went the world fell silent and her hair coiled in slow motion so as to sear the image into Elias's mind, her eyes closing and the faint scent of jasmine lingering there on the edge so as to further wound him and bring forth that solitary scarlet tear. Then she was gone.

He felt the rays of the sun as they broke the horizon and cut across the sky like innumerable swords, their silver blades racing from the fires that shaped them and then he pulled the hand to him. There was the gray light as it filtered in the sky. He thought of Echo then as he slithered back, back towards the corner. In his mind he saw her falling, saw her gray body and the hoary wisps, like trails of incense smoke, coiling upwards towards the sky and towards oblivion.

"What have you done? You fool," Videl bellowed.

But, Elias sank further back into the shadows as the image of Echo fell over him and he saw that beautiful creature strike the barge below, her body erupting into a winding cloud of smoke and ash and then the looking glass struck the empty deck. The glass of the mirror shattered as it landed face down, the pieces scattering about the planks of wood, each of them glistening like fragments of diamonds in the new day. The smoke lifted soft and opaque into the air, thinning as it went, like a bewitched cloud that had been held to the earth and now was free to wind its way back into the atmosphere from which it came.

In the light Videl groaned. There was a rattle in his voice and then he choked. He looked as though time were streaming past him while the frame of his corpse stood motionless in space. The eyeballs in his head became protuberant, like two crazed things trying to be born from his sockets. The wraith tried to move, to clutch blindly at Elias, but his remains just crashed to the wood slats and rail spikes of the tracks. Worms and insects scurried and reeled in the bone pile, a contiguous glut of decomposers that had somehow been conjured together to form his hideous frame. Now that ponderous anatomy glistened beside the stovepipe hat as the sunlight gleaned from the skull and the marrow and threw itself towards the dilated eyes of Elias Dumont.

He crouched in the darkness. With his life rushing through his mind, he balled himself up like a grimacing fetus and all of his cruelty and careless behavior was restored to him. He knew the pain of his vanities as the nose left his body and the skullish cavity formed and he understood his self abuses as the cancers came and bulged upon him so that his ape like body was mounded with malignant swells. A leathery hand sought the tumors upon his head and face and then the fingers trembled through his hair.

The Reflection of Elias Dumont

Then the image of Aurore came, like a visage sent to torment him. It replayed in his mind in crystal definition. He saw his hands around her neck and the silvery stains upon her face, stains from the river of tears that flooded in her eyes, drowning out that horrible look of questioning as they spilled over her cheeks. He recalled the taste of her skin as he kissed her that last time and his tears bled into hers and ran until they stood glistening over the bruises on her neck, the blacking shapes of his fingers that stood out like crows upon a field of pale blue snow.

Elias moaned, the memory of her in his arms swept into his thoughts, of her billowing white dress with its hand stitched flowers and the flowing wedding train soiled as it dragged upon the ground. He saw again the flowers around her hair and the gossamer veil that she had blushed beneath just hours before she had found the mirror and his ruinous hands had found her throat. There was nothing for him but that image now as he crouched there, just as he had crouched then, pulling the veil back over Aurore's eyes and easing her into the dark brown water of the river and then kneeling as he watched her drift silently away.

Muttering to himself, Elias stood up then and ran. Each window of light seared his flesh as he made his way down the terminal until he reached the opening of the tunnel. He could hear the voices of people in the distance as they entered the station. In the rail he could feel the vibration of the train and he wrung his hands as the unstoppable feeling of sleep or death drove upon him. There was a stairwell in that darkness and from it came the smell of moisture and decay.

The old iron stairwell had been clumsily roped off with caution tape and in the panic of his situation and the haste that defined him Elias tore away the yellow plastic and descended, with a heavy heart and a heavier foot, the flight of creaking steps. The city itself in its ever awakened state did not take notice. The cyclist pedaled by the station in his state of self concern and the business people in their suits and ties walked with their briefcases and cell phones and the cabby's sat waiting to earn a fare and every man woman and child with their own interests went about the routines of their lives.

He made it no more than the first turn of the spiral case before it groaned and shifted like the bones of something long dead who now, being trodden upon, were reanimated, awoken into service from the depths of their tomb and then, in their deteriorated state, buckled and broke loose. No one heard the sound of the anchoring pop, of the rusty railing split and snap, of the twisting metal as it crashed in the darkness. No one heard his scream as he plunged into the leg of the bridge, with the train rustling by and the sun burning full over the arched horizon, burning in the smear of chalk blue sky like all the worlds selfish desire across the dark brown surface of the river, a long band of flame that danced across the particles of silt, particles of things that once were. But now the dark water flowed and broke them down, depositing these elemental forms so they may sleep in the earth, awaiting their time to rise again.

The Reflection of Elias Dumont

J L Carey Jr. is a writer and an artist living in Michigan with his wife and three children. He is an Instructor of English and Art and holds an MFA in Creative Writing from National University and a BA in English from the University of Michigan with a concentration in writing. He has had various stories and poems published in both print and online journals.

Other books by J L Carey Jr:
Turning Pages, poems 2010
Callous, In Spring Selected Poems 2013
Repressions Poems 2015
Songs of Epigenesis Poems 2016

The Reflection of Elias Dumont